Bobby grabbed my sleeve and looked me in the eye.

"Stoshack," he said. "I didn't come over here to blackmail you."

"Then why *did* you come over?" I asked.

"I need you to take me back in time."

I just stared at him.

"Are you crazy?" I finally said.

No way was I going to take that lunatic back in time with me. I almost got killed a few times doing it myself. With Bobby Fuller along for the ride, there was no telling what might happen, what could go wrong.

"Stoshack," Bobby said, "I need to meet Jim Thorpe."

Also by Dan Gutman

The Get Rich Quick Club
Johnny Hangtime
Casey Back at Bat

Baseball Card Adventures:

Honus & Me
Jackie & Me
Babe & Me
Shoeless Joe & Me
Mickey & Me
Abner & Me
Satch & Me

My Weird School:

Miss Daisy Is Crazy!
Mr. Klutz Is Nuts!
Mrs. Roopy Is Loopy!
Ms. Hannah Is Bananas!
Miss Small Is off the Wall!
Mr. Hynde Is Out of His Mind!
Mrs. Cooney Is Loony!
Ms. LaGrange Is Strange!
Miss Lazar Is Bizarre!
Mr. Docker Is off His Rocker!
Mrs. Kormel Is Not Normal!
Ms. Todd Is Odd!
Mrs. Patty Is Batty!
Miss Holly Is Too Jolly!
Mr. Macky Is Wacky!

Ms. Coco Is Loco!
Miss Suki Is Kooky!
Mrs. Yonkers Is Bonkers!
Dr. Carbles Is Losing His Marbles!
Mr. Louie Is Screwy!
Ms. Krup Cracks Me Up!
Mrs. Dole Is Out of Control!
Mr. Sunny Is Funny!
Mr. Granite Is from Another Planet!
Coach Hyatt Is a Riot!
Officer Spence Makes No Sense!
Mrs. Jafee Is Daffy!
Dr. Brad Has Gone Mad!
Miss Laney Is Zany!

JIM
& Me

A Baseball Card Adventure

Dan Gutman

HARPER

An Imprint of HarperCollins*Publishers*

Library of Congress Cataloging-in-Publication Data
Gutman, Dan.
    Jim & me : a baseball card adventure / Dan Gutman. — 1st ed.
        p.   cm.
    Summary: Joe and his longtime enemy, Bobby Fuller, use a vintage baseball card to travel in time,
hoping to stop Jim Thorpe from participating in the 1912 Olympics and losing his medals, but instead
they watch Thorpe struggle during his first season with the New York Giants.
    ISBN 978-0-06-059496-1
    1. Thorpe, Jim, 1887–1953—Juvenile fiction. [1. Thorpe, Jim, 1887–1953—Fiction. 2. Baseball—
Fiction. 3. Athletes—Fiction. 4. Indians of North America—Fiction. 5. Time travel—Fiction.] I. Title.
II. Title: Jim and me.
PZ7.G9846Jim 2008   2007030703
[Fic]—dc22   CIP
                                                                                                  AC

Typography by Chlöé Foglia
10 11 12 13 14   CG/CW   10 9 8 7 6 5 4 3 2
❖
First paperback edition, 2010

To Rachel Orr and Barbara Lalicki
and all the good folks at HarperCollins
who have been so supportive

Acknowledgments

This book would have been impossible to complete without the generous help of David Kelly of the Library of Congress, Ryan Chamberlain of the Society for American Baseball Research, and Bill Francis, Jeff Arnett, and Pat Kelly of the National Baseball Hall of Fame. Special thanks to Zach Rice for his encyclopedic knowledge of baseball cards, Steve Chorney and my wife, Nina, for their artwork, Irv Klubeck for his football expertise, and Howard Wolf for helping me find the site of the old Polo Grounds.

Sir, you are the greatest athlete in the world!
—King Gustav V of Sweden, upon meeting
Jim Thorpe at the Olympics in July 1912

Show me a hero and I will write you a tragedy.
—F. Scott Fitzgerald

1

Games of Deception

"SEE THE BALL. HIT THE BALL," OUR COACH, FLIP
Valentini, was telling the guys when I skidded my
bike up to the dugout at Dunn Field. "Catch it.
Throw it. And show up on time or you don't play. It's
a simple game, boys."

Flip ought to know. He pitched for the Brooklyn
Dodgers in their glory years. He was with
Cincinnati and Pittsburgh too for a while. Flip won
287 games and struck out almost 3,000 batters
during his career. He's in the Baseball Hall of Fame.

But Flip wasn't always famous. He used to be
just a plain old guy who owned Flip's Fan Club, a
baseball card shop here in Louisville. He coached
our team in his spare time. But then Flip and I did
something crazy one day. We traveled back to 1942
with a radar gun. We wanted to see if we could clock
the speed of a Satchel Paige fastball. While we were

back there, Satch taught Flip a few trick pitches. I had to leave Flip in 1942, and he got to live his life all over again. So when I returned to the twenty-first century, Flip was famous.

Oh, yeah. I can travel through time. I'll get to that in a few minutes.

I was sure that Flip was going to stop coaching our team after he was inducted into the Hall of Fame. Why should a famous guy like him bother with a bunch of kids like us? But he just loves the game and won't give it up.

Anyway, I parked my bike and Flip winked at me even though I was a few minutes late. The other team hadn't shown up yet. While the guys and I huddled around Flip, I kept looking around.

"Who are we playing today?" I asked.

"Your favorite team, Stosh," Flip said. "The Exterminators."

"Oh, no!" we all groaned.

"Do we have to play them *again*?" asked Phillip Rollison, our shortstop.

"I told their coach I wanted a rematch," Flip said. WHAT?!

"Those guys are murder!" said Kevin Cordiero, who plays first base for us.

The Exterminators are this weird team sponsored by a Louisville company that kills bugs . . . and other Little League teams. They've got a roach for a mascot. They also have this tall left-hander named

Kyle who we nicknamed Mutant Man because the kid is virtually unhittable. He throws like 80 miles an hour. We were lucky to score a run off him the last time we played.

"Fuhgetaboutit," Flip said. "I got a plan to beat 'em this time."

We were all pretty P.O.'d that we had to face the Exterminators again, but we forgot about it once the game started. The nice thing was that the Exterminators didn't start Kyle the Mutant. Maybe he was tired or something. He was sitting on the bench spitting sunflower seeds.

Without Kyle on the mound, the Exterminators were still a good team. We were playing them pretty evenly, and they only had us by a run going into the sixth inning. That's the last inning in our league.

We were getting ready to come to bat in the bottom of the sixth when *guess who* walked out to the mound to warm up.

"Oh, no!" we all groaned. "They're bringing in the Mutant!"

The Exterminators wanted to shut the door on us so we couldn't tie it up in the bottom of the sixth. Kyle's first warm-up pitch sizzled across the plate. I could hear it hiss before it exploded into the catcher's mitt. And the guy hadn't even loosened up yet!

"We're finished," moaned Phillip. "Might as well start packing up the gear."

"Relax," Flip said as he stepped out of the

3

dugout. "I told ya I got a plan."

"Maybe Flip can hit this guy," said Kevin, "but I know I can't."

Flip is really old—in his eighties, I think. When he shuffled out of the dugout, the umpire came over so Flip wouldn't have to walk too far. Flip took a piece of paper out of his pocket.

"Excuse me, Jack," Flip said to the ump. "Can I have a word with you?"

"Whatcha got there, Mr. V?" asked the ump.

"A birth certificate," Flip said, handing him the paper.

"Tryin' to show me how young you are, Flip?"

"It's not *my* birth certificate, you bonehead," Flip said good-naturedly. "It's *his* birth certificate."

Flip pointed at Kyle the Mutant, who stopped his warm-up pitch just as he was about to release the ball. Everybody looked at him. The Exterminators' coach came running out to see what was going on.

"Is there a problem here?" the coach asked.

"The problem is that your pitcher is fifteen years old," Flip told him. "If I'm not mistaken, this league is for kids who are fourteen and younger."

"Lemme see that!" the coach said, grabbing the paper.

The three of them gathered together, examining the birth certificate. Finally the ump walked over to Kyle, who was standing on the mound with his hands on his hips.

"Son, how old are you?" the umpire asked.

"I just turned fifteen yesterday," Kyle said.

"Happy birthday," said the ump, "but you can't play in this league anymore."

Well, it was like Christmas and New Year's and the last day of school all wrapped up in one. We all started whooping and hollering on the bench. Kyle the Mutant handed the ball to the ump and slinked off the field. His coach ran desperately up and down their bench trying to find somebody who could pitch the last inning. Flip shuffled back to our dugout and we all got down on our knees and did the "we're not worthy" thing.

"How'd you get the Mutant Man's birth certificate, Flip?" Kevin asked.

"I got my sources," he replied.

We were so happy, we almost forgot that we still had to score another run just to tie the game. I was due to bat fourth, so somebody had to get on base for me to get my ups.

A few minutes went by before a kid came out of the Exterminator's dugout and walked to the mound. I looked him over. The kid was short. I didn't recognize him.

"I know that guy," said our catcher, Carlos Montano. "He's in my math class."

"What's he throw?" asked Phillip.

"Junk," replied Carlos. "He doesn't throw hard."

We watched the kid's every move as he warmed up. A righty. He was throwing curveballs. But not the kind of curves that bite into the air and change

5

direction like they're ricocheting off a wall. Nice, big, lazy curveballs. The kid was just lobbing them in.

I licked my lips. I couldn't hit Kyle the Mutant. But I could hit this kid any day. I *feast* on curveballs. And this kid didn't even have a good one.

If you ask me, the curveball is what makes baseball different from other sports. Look at it this way: In basketball, you have to be tall. In football, you have to be big. But a skinny little kid who can throw or hit a curve has it all over a big, strong doofus who can't. That's because baseball doesn't require height or weight. It's a game of deception.

When I was little, my dad taught me everything about curveballs. It's all physics. You see, a baseball isn't smooth. It has 216 stitches. You grip the ball along the stitches and twist your wrist as you release it. The ball spins, and the stitches bump against the air. The air becomes turbulent. It's sort of like a little tornado around the ball. So there's less air pressure on one side of the ball than on the other, and it curves.

Anyway, I got to be pretty good at hitting curves. If I had bigger hands, I would be able to throw a wicked curve too. You need to put a lot of spin on the ball. The more spin, the more curve. I guess that's why I'm not a pitcher.

We all edged forward on the bench. Owen Jones led off for us, and we were hollering for him to get a hit.

"Save my ups, Owen!" I yelled.

The first pitch was in the dirt, but Owen took a cut at the next one and sliced a scorcher down the third base line. By the time the Exterminators got the ball in, Owen was sliding into third with a triple.

Our bench went nuts. Man on third, nobody out. All we needed was a single, a sacrifice fly, an error, or a passed ball. It would be a cinch to get Owen home and tie it up. And the way this guy pitched, we could probably win it too.

Carlos was up next. I guess he was a little over-anxious, because he took a big rip at the first pitch and topped a little dribbler back to the mound. The pitcher looked the runner back to third and threw to first. One out.

That's okay. Kevin was our next batter, and he could hit. I put on a helmet and grabbed my bat. I was on deck.

"Drive me in, Kev!" shouted Owen from third base.

Flip told Kevin to wait for a good pitch and he worked the count to 2 and 2. Nothing but lazy curve-balls. On the next pitch, Kevin swung and we all knew instantly he'd hit it a long way. We stood up to watch the flight of the ball as it rocketed down the rightfield line toward the trees.

"Foul ball!" the ump yelled. If Kevin had hit the ball a foot or two to the left, it would have been a home run. Two runs would have scored, and the game would be over.

"Nobody hits a ball that hard twice in one at-bat," Flip muttered on our bench.

He was right, as usual. On the next pitch, Kevin bounced out to short. Owen scampered back to third rather than risk getting thrown out at the plate.

Two outs. My turn.

"Go get 'em, Stosh," Flip hollered as I walked up to the plate. "You're our last chance."

I dug my heel into the box and pumped my bat across the plate a few times. The pitcher looked nervous. I tried to remember everything my dad told me about hitting curveballs.

The first pitch came in and I took a wild swing at the ball, but it clicked off my bat and smashed into the backstop behind me. Strike one. I should have *killed* that pitch.

Relax! You're overanxious, I told myself. *Just try for a single.*

"You can do it, Stosh!" somebody yelled from our dugout.

The next pitch was high. Or at least I thought it was high. The umpire called it a strike. I could have argued, but I know from experience that arguing with umps is a waste of time.

"Get some glasses!" somebody yelled from the bleachers.

Two strikes. Now I had to protect the plate. No way I was going to strike out looking. Not against *this* kid. He threw *so* slow. It was like a beach ball floating to the plate. I was determined to go after anything close.

The pitcher looked in for a sign. I pumped the bat

a few more times. With an 0-2 count, he might waste one off the outside corner and try to make me go fishing for it. *Don't take that bait.* I tried to peek behind me to see where the catcher was setting up his target.

"See the ball. Hit the ball," Flip yelled.

The pitcher wound up and I got ready. *Wait for it,* I told myself. *Don't be overanxious.*

His arm came down and I saw the ball leave his hand. But it was coming in harder than his other pitches. He crossed me up! He was throwing me a fastball! It may not have been that fast, but it was a lot faster than his curve. I tried to adjust and get my bat on it, maybe foul it off.

Too late. I hit air.

"Strike three!" the ump yelled. "That's the ball game, boys."

The Exterminators went nuts. Their stupid roach mascot started dancing around the infield. I dragged my bat back to the bench, steam coming out of my ears. Everybody said the right things. *Forget about it, Stosh. Nice try, Stosh. We'll get 'em next time, Stosh.* All those things you say to a teammate after he whiffs *with the tying run at third.*

Sometimes life throws you a curveball. And just when you're expecting the curve, life throws you a fastball. Life is a lot like baseball. You never know what to expect.

Come to think of it, they're *both* games of deception.

2

An Unexpected Guest

I RODE MY BIKE HOME AFTER THE GAME. SOMETIMES Mom picks me up, but she wasn't sure if she could get to the field on time. Mom's a nurse at Louisville Hospital and she works late a lot. As I rolled my bike in the garage, she was just pulling into the driveway.

"How was the game, Joey?" Mom asked.

"I hit a grand salami to win it in extra innings," I lied.

"For real?"

"Actually, we lost," I admitted. "I don't want to talk about it."

Mom told me to wash up for dinner. I asked her if we could go out to eat, knowing full well she'd say no. We don't have a lot of money, especially since my mom and dad split up. Anything other than fast food is a "special occasion."

I was washing my hands when the doorbell rang.

Mom shot me a look that said I should go answer it. She was afraid it was my dad, and she never wants to talk to him if she can avoid it. Dad and I get together about once a week, but he usually calls first and I ride my bike over to his apartment.

I went to see who it was while Mom scurried upstairs to hide.

Well, when I opened the door, the last person in the world I'd expect to see was standing there— Bobby Fuller.

Now, let me tell you a little about this kid. Bobby Fuller is a bad guy. It's as simple as that. He's a psycho, a liar, and a kleptomaniac. (That's somebody who steals.) In fourth grade he shot some kid in the leg with a BB gun. In fifth grade he was suspended for cursing out a teacher. I heard that one of his uncles killed himself a few years ago. Bobby probably has some mental problem and takes medication for it. I sure hope so anyway.

Bobby is a big guy, a little bigger than me. He's in my grade at school, and he used to play baseball in my league too. Ever since our T-ball days, he has hated me. I never knew why. When he was pitching, he'd throw the ball at my head. When he was playing the infield, he'd try to trip me as I was running the bases. When he was playing the outfield, he would shout insults to try to distract me. The guy is just *bad*, and I try to steer clear of him. I was so relieved when I heard that Bobby Fuller gave up baseball and switched to football.

Bobby wasn't in any of my classes this year, and I hadn't seen him in a while. I had no idea why he would be standing at my front door. He must be raising money for his football team, I figured. Probably selling candy bars or something.

I stepped out onto the porch because I really didn't want Bobby in my house. He would probably steal something or make a rude remark to my mom. I didn't even feel comfortable with Bobby Fuller knowing where I lived.

"What's up?" I said cautiously. I didn't want to be a jerk or anything and slam the door in his face. But then again, I didn't want to act overly friendly either.

"Nothin'," Bobby muttered.

So why are you standing here? I thought. He looked uncomfortable, like he had something to say but didn't know how to start. I tried to meet Bobby's eyes, but he kept looking away. I wished Mom would interrupt and call me in for dinner or something.

"How come you gave up baseball?" I asked, for lack of anything better to say.

"Baseball is for wimps," he replied. "In football, they let you hit guys."

I thought about telling him that football is for muscle-bound morons who don't have the brains to think, but I decided against it. You don't disturb a beehive unless you want to get stung.

"Why not play hockey?" I suggested. "*They* let you hit guys too."

"I can't skate," Bobby said. "Listen, Stoshack, I need to talk to you."

Aha! The real reason why he came over.

"About what?"

"I know your little secret," Bobby said in a low voice.

I rolled my eyes. Here we go. I knew this day would come. It was only a matter of time before Bobby would try to blackmail me.

There are only a small number of people who know my secret. Bobby happens to be one of them. And now you are too.

My secret is that I can travel through time.

Oh, I know. You've seen it all before. You probably saw *Back to the Future* or read *The Time Machine* by H. G. Wells. People are always traveling through time in stories. But I can *really* do it—with baseball cards.

It all started when I was little. I would pick up one of my dad's old baseball cards and feel this strange tingling sensation in my fingertips. It was like they were vibrating or something.

I didn't think much about it, until one day I found an old card while I was cleaning out the attic for this lady named Amanda Young. I held the card in my hand and closed my eyes. The next thing I knew, I was back in 1909. Baseball cards sort of act like a plane ticket for me, and they take me to the year on the card.

Scientists say time travel is impossible. But what

do they know? I've *done* it. For me, time is like a video. You can rewind it or fast-forward it. I swear I'm not making this stuff up. I'm not some crackpot who hallucinates that I've been abducted by aliens.

But if word got around that I could travel through time, people might think I was a little strange. So I haven't exactly advertised the fact that I have this "special" power. A few people know: You. My parents. My coach, Flip. My Uncle Wilbur. My cousin Samantha. That's how Bobby Fuller found out. Samantha can't keep her big mouth shut, and she happens to be in the same class as Bobby's little sister.

But you know what? I don't care anymore. I'm tired of keeping my secret. So I can travel through time. Big deal. It's not like I'm a criminal or anything. I'm just a little different from other kids. It's sort of like having red hair or being left-handed. Nothing to be ashamed of.

"Go ahead. Tell anybody you want," I told Bobby. "Knock yourself out."

Maybe that would make him go away. If I didn't keep it a secret, then he couldn't use it against me. I turned around to go back inside the house.

But Bobby didn't go away. He grabbed my sleeve and looked me in the eye.

"Stoshack," he said. "I didn't come over here to blackmail you."

"Then why *did* you come over?" I asked.

"I need you to take me back in time."

I just stared at him.

"Are you crazy?" I finally said.

No way was I going to take that lunatic back in time with me. I almost got killed a few times doing it myself. With Bobby Fuller along for the ride, there was no telling what might happen, what could go wrong.

"Stoshack," Bobby said, "I need to meet Jim Thorpe."

JIM THORPE?

Who's Jim Thorpe? I searched my memory for the name. Jim Thorpe wasn't a baseball player, that I knew of anyway. And I know a lot about baseball history. I have a collection of baseball books, and I've read them all. I know the name of just about every player in *The Baseball Encyclopedia*.

But that name *was* familiar. Jim Thorpe may have been a pro football player, it seemed to me. And I thought he had something to do with the Olympics a long time ago. One of the kids in my class did a report on him a while back. I didn't remember any details.

"Who's Jim Thorpe?" I finally asked.

"Only the greatest athlete of the twentieth century," Bobby told me.

"And he played *baseball*?"

"Sure, he played baseball!" Bobby insisted.

"How do *you* know?" I asked.

Bobby is probably the dumbest kid in our whole

school. I heard he flunked *gym* last year, and I have no idea what you have to do to flunk gym.

"I read a book about him," Bobby said.

Bobby Fuller read a book? Now, *that* was a shocker.

"So why do you want to meet him so badly?" I asked.

"Jim Thorpe was my great-grandfather."

3

Bobby Fuller's Secret

I SAT DOWN ON THE STEPS, AND BOBBY SAT DOWN NEXT to me. Bobby Fuller was related to Jim Thorpe? Who knew? He never mentioned it before. It wasn't one of those things that everybody talked about at school.

Before Bobby could tell me anything else, the screen door opened and my mom came out.

"Robert Fuller!" she said, looking just as surprised as I had when Bobby showed up at the door. Mom recognized Bobby right away because of all the times I played baseball against him. She knew the horrible things he did and said to me over the years too.

"Hello, Mrs. Stoshack," Bobby said pleasantly, shaking her hand. Like a lot of bad guys, he knew how to act like a little angel when he was around grown-ups. That way, the grown-ups didn't know what a jerk he was.

I figured my mom would probably slap Bobby across the face or call the police. But when all is said and done, she's still a mom.

"Would you like some cookies?" she asked.

Why is it that we never have any cookies in the house when *I* want some, but they always magically appear whenever company comes over? And how come *I'm* not allowed to eat cookies before dinner, but it's okay when company comes over before dinner?

Anyway, I wasn't going to complain. Mom went inside and came out with a huge plate full of chocolate-chip cookies. Bobby and I each took two.

I could tell my mom was dying to know why Bobby was there, but I threw her a look that said we needed privacy. She scurried back into the house, leaving the plate of cookies with us. I knew she'd pump me for details later.

"Jim Thorpe was a Native American," Bobby said when the door slammed shut. I guess I looked puzzled, so he added, "an Indian."

"Yeah, I knew that," I said, not all that convincingly.

"He had seven kids, and one of his daughters was my grandma," Bobby continued. "She died when I was little, so I don't remember her. But I'm one-eighth Sac and Fox Indian."

Bobby Fuller was part Indian? He didn't look Indian. I figured he was Irish or German or something.

"That's cool," I said, and it was. I wish I was related to somebody famous. "How come you don't tell everybody?"

"Tell people I have Indian blood?" Bobby said. "I don't *think* so."

"What, is there prejudice against Indians?" I asked.

Bobby looked at me like I was an idiot so I didn't press it. I know we've come a long way, but there's still a lot of prejudice in the world. White kids don't often see it because it doesn't affect us directly. So we assume it doesn't exist.

"Stoshack," Bobby said. "I want to meet my great-grandfather."

Well, I'll be honest with you. I didn't want to do it. Time travel is not an exact science. It's not like I could step inside some time machine, push a few buttons, and *poof*—I would magically appear in Jim Thorpe's living room. There are usually some complications, to put it mildly. I could get *killed*.

One time, I went back to 1919 to try to prevent the Black Sox scandal. I ended up getting kidnapped, tied to a chair, and shot at.

Another time, I went back to 1863 with my mom to see if Abner Doubleday really invented baseball. But we landed in the middle of the Battle of Gettysburg during the Civil War, with a bunch of Confederate soldiers shooting at us.

And that time when Flip and I went back to 1942

to see Satchel Paige, some guy tried to shoot us because his daughter fell in love with Flip.

Come to think of it, I've been shot at a lot.

The point is, if I'm going to use my power to go back in time, I've got to have a really good reason. I won't risk my life just for the fun of it or to meet some famous baseball player.

Besides, why should I do any favors for Bobby Fuller? What did he ever do for me? He's been tormenting me since our T-ball days. It's not *my* job to help arrange his family reunions.

It was obvious that the only reason Bobby was suddenly being nice to me and my mom was because he wanted a favor.

"I know you don't like me, Stoshack," Bobby said.

He got no argument from me there. Bobby reached into his jeans pocket and pulled out a wad of crumpled bills. There were some tens and twenties in there. He might have had a hundred dollars or more. I didn't even want to guess what illegal thing he had done to get that much money. But he held it out to me.

"Here."

"You'll *pay* me to take you back in time to meet Jim Thorpe?" I asked.

"Yeah," Fuller said, "like you'd pay a cab driver to take you someplace."

I'm not a cab driver. I didn't take the cash. If I went back in time with Bobby Fuller and got hurt—or even killed—his money wouldn't do me any good.

My life is worth more than a hundred bucks.

But there was another reason I didn't take the cash. Even if I'd wanted to help Bobby, I couldn't.

"I'm sorry," I told him, "but in order to go back in time to meet Jim Thorpe, I would have to have a Jim Thorpe baseball card. And I don't even know if there WERE any Jim Thorpe baseball cards."

And with that, Fuller reached into his pocket and handed me this:

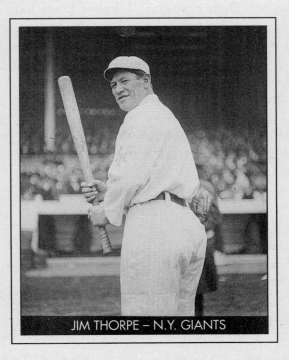

JIM THORPE – N.Y. GIANTS

I started to feel that tingling sensation in my fingertips.

The card was worn and wrinkled. Probably not worth much in that condition. But as I held it in my hand, I started to feel that faint tingling sensation. It was sort of like the feeling you get when you touch a TV screen. It didn't hurt. It was a pleasant feeling.

"This card has been in my family for years," Bobby said.

The tingling got stronger, and in a few more seconds my whole hand felt like it was vibrating. Then my wrist. Then my arm. I knew from experience that if I held on any longer, I would reach the point of no return.

I dropped the card.

"Let me think about it," I told Bobby.

"Think hard, Stoshack," he said. "This is important."

He snatched the last cookie off the plate before I could get it, jumped down the steps, and walked away.

4

Pros and Cons

WHENEVER I WANT TO IMPRESS MY TEACHERS AT SCHOOL, I use the word "ambivalent." It's a great word because most kids don't know what it means.

Well, I'll tell you what it means so you can use it at school and impress *your* teachers. It means having mixed feelings. Like when you can't make up your mind about something and it really tears you apart. This is a problem I seem to have a lot.

When Bobby Fuller asked me to take him back in time to meet Jim Thorpe, I promised him I'd think it over. So I did.

Before I made any decision one way or another, I figured I'd better get some information. The Louisville Library is just a couple of miles from my house, so I hopped on my bike the next day after school and rode over there.

Yeah, I know the Internet is easier. I could have

just Googled "Jim Thorpe" and found a zillion websites about him. But I like to look through books. I like the feeling of paper on my fingers. Maybe I'm old-fashioned. And I get sick of staring at a screen all the time. It hurts my eyes.

Anyway, there's only one number in the Dewey Decimal System that I know by heart—796. That's the number for sports. If you walk into any library in America and go to 796 in the nonfiction section, you'll find a shelf or two of sports books.

I scanned the shelves until I found some books about the greatest athletes of all time. If Jim Thorpe was as amazing as Fuller said he was, he should be in there, right?

Well, what I found was a little bit suprising. Not only did Jim Thorpe play major-league baseball, but he also played professional football. So I was right! In fact, he was one of the original members of the Football Hall of Fame. But the most interesting thing was that Thorpe didn't become famous for playing baseball *or* football. He became famous because, in the 1912 Olympics, he won gold medals in the decathlon and the pentathlon.

I didn't even know what those events were at first, so I looked them up in a book about the Olympics. In the decathlon, it said, athletes compete in ten different track-and-field events, everything from sprinting to pole vaulting to throwing the javelin. So the winner of the Olympic decathlon is considered to be the best all-around athlete in the world. The pentathlon, which isn't in the Olympics anymore, was made up of five other events. Thorpe won that too.

These days, hardly any pro athletes play more than one sport. Most of them specialize, and many even specialize *within* their sport. Like in baseball they've got "closers," whose job is to come in and pitch just one inning. They've got designated hitters who don't have to play the field. In football they've got guys who *only* punt, or do nothing but return punts.

But Jim Thorpe did it *all*—baseball, football, plus all those track-and-field events. He must have been like Superman in his time.

I know a lot about sports, but I had no idea how great Jim Thorpe was. It didn't make sense that somebody who was that good wasn't more famous. Why hadn't I heard about this guy before?

Then I got to a part in the book that caught my eye:

". . . seven months after his Olympic triumph, it was discovered that Jim Thorpe was not an amateur athlete, as the rules required. He had played semi-pro baseball for two summers before the Olympics, earning as little as two dollars per game. Thorpe was forced to return his Olympic medals."

What?! The guy was the greatest athlete in the world and they took his Olympic medals away because he made a few bucks playing baseball? Wow.

That was unbelievable. Jim Thorpe really got screwed over.

Maybe I'm dumb or something, but I didn't even know there was a day when professional athletes weren't allowed to compete in the Olympics. I mean, pros are in the Olympics all the time now. You see NBA "dream teams" playing Olympic basketball. You see NHL stars playing Olympic hockey. You see Olympic athletes in TV commercials. They have to be getting paid. How else could they afford to train so hard for four years if they don't get paid? What are they supposed to do for money, deliver pizzas?

I always thought the Olympics were about being the *best*, not being the best amateur or the best professional. It shouldn't matter who you are.

The New York Times

NEW YORK, TUESDAY, JANUARY 28, 1913. — TWENTY-TWO PAGES.

OLYMPIC PRIZES LOST; THORPE NO AMATEUR

Carlisle School Indian Admits He Once Played Professional Baseball in the South.

DIDN'T REALIZE HIS DECEIT

Our Committee Must Return Decathlon Cup and Pentathlon Trophy, Reducing Our Points from 85 to 80.

James Thorpe, a Sac and Fox Indian student of the Carlisle Indian School, confessed to the Amateur Athletic Union officials yesterday that he had played professional baseball in 1909 and 1910, thereby automatically disqualifying himself for any amateur competition since the Summer of 1909.

There was an old newspaper article about Jim Thorpe printed in the book. I made a photocopy in case I might need it later.

All kinds of thoughts were running through my head as I sat down with the book. Maybe Bobby Fuller was hoping he could warn Thorpe about what was going to happen to him. Maybe he was hoping he could save Jim Thorpe's reputation, and make his great-grandfather a hero again. Return the glory to his family, and to all American Indians. Maybe Bobby wanted to go back in time and change history.

And I was the only one who could help him.

I was feeling . . . well, ambivalent. And when I'm feeling ambivalent, I'll tell you what I do. I take a sheet of paper and put a line down the middle. I write PRO on one side of the line and CON on the other. Then I try to figure out which side of the paper deserves to win.

PRO	CON
• Could be fun	• Would have to take Bobby back in time with me
• Meet the greatest athlete ever	
• Help Bobby	• Hate Bobby
	• Could get hurt or even killed
	• Could change history for the worse

I thought about that last point on the PRO side. It was a long shot, but maybe if Bobby went back in time and met his great-grandfather it would turn him around as a person, help him solve his personal problems. Maybe he wouldn't be so angry at the world. And then maybe he wouldn't be so angry at *me*.

I looked over my sheet of PROS and CONS and asked myself if one side outweighed the other. There was no clear winner. I was leaning toward the CON side, but I was still ambivalent.

"The library will be closing in 15 minutes," the librarian announced over the loudspeaker.

I put the books away and rode my bike home.

My mother was putting dinner out when I opened the kitchen door. Uncle Wilbur was at the table waiting to eat. He's really old, even older than Flip.

"Wash your hands, Joey," said Uncle Wilbur.

"Where were you?" asked my mother.

"At the library," I told her.

"Doing homework?"

"Not exactly," I admitted.

After I washed up, I told them what I'd learned about Jim Thorpe. Uncle Wilbur said he remembered Thorpe as a football player, but even *he* was too young to remember the 1912 Olympics.

"I don't trust that Fuller boy," Mom said as she put some vegetables on my plate. "What if you two go back in time and he steals your baseball card? You'll have no way to get home. You'll be stuck in the past forever. Did you think about that?"

She was right. And it hadn't crossed my mind.

"I wouldn't put it past him," I said.

Uncle Wilbur sighed and we looked at him. Oh yeah. If I didn't have the power to travel through time, I wouldn't even *have* an Uncle Wilbur.

You see, a year ago, my Uncle Wilbur didn't exist. It's true! I was always told that he died as a child in an influenza epidemic that killed millions of people back in 1919. But when I went back to that year to meet Shoeless Joe Jackson, I also met Wilbur when he was a boy. I had some flu medicine with me and I gave it to him. When I came back to the present day, Uncle Wilbur was alive. So I guess the medicine saved his life. It was a happy accident.

"What do I always tell you to do when you get a lemon?" Uncle Wilbur asked.

"Make lemonade," I replied.

"Right," he said. "And what do I always tell you to do when life throws you a curve?"

"Hit it," I replied.

"That's right," Uncle Wilbur said. "Hit it *hard*."

At some moment in time you have to stop *thinking* about whether or not you should do something and just *do* it. So I decided I would take Bobby Fuller back in time to meet Jim Thorpe. I would do it for Bobby's sake, even though he was a world-class jerk. My good deed for the day. For a lifetime, really.

After dinner, I cleared off the table and helped my mom wash the dishes. Then I looked up Bobby

Fuller's phone number in the school directory and called him.

"Did you think about what I asked you?" Bobby said as soon as he recognized my voice.

"Yeah," I replied. "Come on over."

5

That Old Tingling Sensation

WHEN BOBBY SHOWED UP AT OUR FRONT DOOR A FEW minutes later, he had a backpack slung over one shoulder.

"Look," I told him, "this isn't going to be an overnight thing, okay? We're going to meet Jim Thorpe and come right back. It will be 15 minutes, tops. In and out. You got that?"

"Relax, Stoshack," Bobby said. "I like to have my stuff with me in case of an emergency."

I poked his backpack. "What've you got in there, anyway?"

"Hey, get your paws off!" Bobby said. "It's my meds, okay? Yeah, I'm ADD. I'm screwed up in the head. Are you happy now, Stoshack?"

Well, I *knew* he was screwed up in the head, but lots of kids have ADD without being psychos.

"The backpack will be a dead giveaway that

we're from the future," I told him. "Kids didn't have backpacks in the old days. We'll want to blend in, not stand out like a couple of freaks."

"You said it would be 15 minutes," Bobby argued. "What's the big deal?"

Man, I hate Bobby Fuller. Something about him always brings out the worst in me. Everything he says just makes me mad. It's the same for him about me, I suppose.

I led Bobby into the living room. My mom was still puttering around the kitchen and I could see her peeking at us through the doorway.

"A little privacy, please?" I said.

Instead of doing what I asked, Mom came and plopped right in the middle of the couch, patting the cushions on either side of her. Bobby and I sat down.

"I just want you boys to know that I expect you to be on your very best behavior," she said. "That means no fighting, no swearing, no drinking, and nothing illegal. You've got to try to get along with each other. Do you understand?"

"Yes, Mom," I said.

"Yes, Mrs. Stoshack," Bobby said.

"And be *careful*!"

"We will," we promised.

She was probably remembering the time I took her back to 1863 and we landed in a graveyard, with bullets and shells exploding all around us. She wasn't too happy about that.

Mom went back to the kitchen and returned

holding two brown paper lunch bags. One was marked BOBBY and the other was marked JOEY.

"In case you need a snack," she said before hurrying upstairs.

It was quiet in the house. Uncle Wilbur had already gone to sleep. Bobby and I sat on the couch. I put my mom's silly lunch bags aside. No way was I taking them with us.

"What do I have to do?" Bobby asked.

"Nothing," I said. "I do the work. You got the card?"

"Yeah," he said, pulling it out of his pocket. I had him put it on the coffee table instead of in my hand. As soon as I touch a card, it sets the wheels in motion for me to go back in time. I wanted to be sure I was ready.

"Okay," I said, "hold my hand."

"What?!" Bobby exclaimed. "Are you kidding? Forget it, Stoshack! I'm not holding hands with you."

"What's your problem?" I said, not really wanting to know the answer.

"I'm not holding hands with a *guy*," he said.

"Look, I don't particularly want to hold hands with you either," I said. "But I can only take somebody with me if we're holding hands. It's sort of like completing an electrical circuit."

"It's *stupid*, is what it is," Bobby said.

"Fine," I told him. "Don't hold hands. I guess we're not going to meet Jim Thorpe after all."

"Okay, okay," said Bobby.

He took my hand like he was picking up some-body's used tissue.

"Oh, wait a minute!" I said, pulling it away.

Suddenly I realized I had forgotten something crucially important—a pack of new baseball cards. Just as an old baseball card would take me to the past, I would need a new baseball card to get me back to the present day. If I went back in time with-out some new cards, I would have no way to get home. I'd be stuck in the past forever.

I bounded upstairs two steps at a time and fished around in my desk until I found a new pack of cards. Then I went back down to the living room. Bobby rolled his eyes.

"Our return ticket," I said, showing him the cards before sticking them in my back pocket.

"You ready now?" Bobby asked. "Let's blow this pop stand."

Bobby took my hand again and I picked the Thorpe card up off the table. It suddenly occurred to me that I hadn't even checked the year of the card. I usually try to research where I'm going before I get there. No time for that now. Oh, well, it would only be 15 minutes anyway.

"What's supposed to happen?" Bobby asked.

"Be patient."

"Nothing's happening," Bobby said after a few seconds.

"Close your eyes," I instructed him. "You'll see."

"How can I see if I close my eyes?" he asked.

"*Shhhh*," I said. "Relax. I need to concentrate."

I closed my eyes and thought about Jim Thorpe. Soon I started feeling the slightest tingling sensation in my fingertips.

"Hey, I think I feel something," Bobby said.

"That means it's working," I whispered.

The tingles buzzed the fingers of my left hand, which were holding the card. I held it tightly so I wouldn't drop it. After a few seconds, I could feel the tingling sensation moving up my wrist and along my arm. It reminds me of a cat's purring.

It was getting stronger, like a wave moving toward the shore.

The tingles washed across my chest and down my legs.

There was no stopping it now.

I couldn't drop the card if I wanted to.

I could feel my body getting lighter.

Molecule by molecule, I was vanishing from the present day.

My whole body was vibrating.

I wanted so badly to open my eyes and watch myself disappear, but I didn't dare.

And then, finally, the wave crashed against the sand. We were gone.

6

Wrong Place, Wrong Time

"WATCH OUT!" BOBBY SCREAMED.

I opened my eyes just in time to see a ball flying right at my head. But it wasn't a baseball. It was about the size of a beach ball. It was black, and it was hanging from a long rope.

Bobby gave me a shove and knocked me over. The ball missed my ear by an inch or two and slammed into a concrete wall behind us. The wall toppled over with a crash, sending pieces of concrete and dust everywhere. I shielded my eyes in case anything else was going to come flying in my direction.

"Are you okay?" I asked Bobby.

"Yeah," he replied. "Where *are* we?"

I looked around, but all I could see were rocks and dirt and rubble everywhere. Oh, no. We must have landed in the middle of another war. But which one?

Then I saw a sign off to my right:

FUTURE SITE OF LOS ANGELES
COUNTY HOSPITAL
Scheduled for completion January 1, 1932

It wasn't a war. We had landed in the middle of a construction site. The ball that had come flying at me was a wrecking ball. They were knocking something down and building a hospital.

Bobby Fuller, of all people, had saved my life.

"You screwed up, Stoshack!" he yelled, brushing the dust off his pants.

"Don't blame *me!*" I yelled right back. "This was *your* stupid idea."

I had to figure this thing out. Jim Thorpe had been in the 1912 Olympics. We were probably in 1931, so it was probably long after his athletic career was over. He had to be retired by now. We messed up somehow. We were in the wrong place at the wrong time.

I looked at Bobby's Jim Thorpe card, which was still in my hand. I wished I had examined the card more closely *before* using it. It didn't look like the style of the cards that were printed at the beginning of the twentieth century. Now, I realized, the card *wasn't* an original from Jim Thorpe's playing days. It was one of those reprints they issue years later. I have some of them in my collection. This one must have been printed in 1931.

"I know what happened," I told Bobby.

"What?"

"I can't just use *any* old baseball card," I told him. "I have to use one from the year I'm trying to *get* to. I always travel back to the year on the card. This card is a reprint from 1931."

"*Now* you tell me!" Bobby shouted. "How was I supposed to know that? Do you think I'm a mind reader?"

"Oh, shut up!" I said. Man, was he annoying.

"You shut up!" Bobby replied. "Let's get out of here before we get killed."

Fine with me. I had better things to do with my time than hang around construction sites in 1931 with Bobby Fuller. I pulled out the new pack of baseball cards I'd stashed in my jeans pocket so we could go home.

I was about to rip open the wrapper when I realized something. Even though the reprint card had taken us to the wrong year, it was still a Jim Thorpe card. So that meant that Jim Thorpe had to be somewhere nearby. Bobby could still meet him. That was all he said he wanted to do in the first place.

"Wait a minute," I said suddenly.

"What's your lame idea now, Stoshack?"

Shoving the cards back in my pocket, I explained the situation to Bobby as I looked around. There were some men in the distance digging with shovels and pouring cement. I saw one guy with his back to us digging a hole in the ground. He was about 50 yards away.

"Maybe that guy can tell us where Jim Thorpe

is," I told Bobby.

"You're nuts," he replied. "These guys are just construction workers. Let's go home."

I walked over to the guy who was shoveling dirt; Bobby followed me. I guess he figured he'd better stick close to me or I might leave him there.

The guy with the shovel was stripped to the waist and his body was shiny with sweat. He looked to be about six feet tall. The muscles in his arms were huge. When he turned to face us, I could see he was a little chubby around the middle. His hair was jet-black, and it flopped over his forehead. He was about forty, I guessed.

"What are you boys doing here?" the guy asked as we approached him. He leaned on his shovel and wiped his face with a rag. "This is a dangerous area."

"Excuse me, mister," I said, "but can you tell us where we might find Jim Thorpe?"

"Jim Thorpe?" the guy asked. "What for?"

"My friend here wants to meet him," I said.

"He's my great-grandfather," added Bobby.

The guy looked Bobby up and down. "You're barkin' up the wrong tree, son. Jim Thorpe doesn't have a great-grandson. He doesn't even have any grandchildren."

"How do you know?" I asked.

"Because I'm Jim Thorpe."

I took a closer look at the guy. He had small brown eyes that nearly disappeared when he squinted at the sun. He had high cheek bones. His skin was a shade darker than mine. But he didn't look like an Indian. At least, he didn't look like the Indians *I'd* seen in movies and on TV. It could have been a suntan, from working outside all day.

"*You're* Jim Thorpe?" I asked in astonishment. "The same Jim Thorpe who won the decathlon in the 1912 Olympics?"

"And the pentathlon."

"Why are you working *here*?" I asked.

I didn't mean to be rude. There's nothing wrong with being a construction worker. But I was used to famous athletes making beer commercials and signing autographs at card shows after their playing days were over. I just didn't think a superstar like Jim Thorpe would be shoveling dirt.

"Lots of men would give their right arm for this job," Thorpe said.

That's when it clicked. 1931. It was the Depression! I remembered when I traveled back in time with my dad to see if Babe Ruth really called his famous "called shot" home run. That was in 1932. There were people all over the streets begging for work and begging for food, struggling to survive.

Bobby Fuller took a step forward.

"Mr. Thorpe," he said, "you probably won't believe this, but we came from the future. I really *am* your great-grandson—or will be, in the twenty-first century."

Jim shook Bobby's hand, looking him square in the eye.

"The Aymara tribe of the high Andes sees the future as behind them and the past as ahead of them," he said. "The past is known, so man sees it in front of him. But man cannot know the future, so he believes it is behind him, where it cannot be seen."

"That's whacked," said Bobby.

Jim Thorpe stared at Bobby, a puzzled look on his face.

"Son, what kind of a knot do you tie when you rope a calf?" Jim asked.

"I don't know," Bobby said.

"How many feet apart do you plant rows of corn?" Jim asked.

"Uh . . . five?" Bobby guessed.

"Tell me what you know about the Black Hawk War," Jim said.

"Never heard of it," Bobby admitted.

Jim sighed, and shook his head sadly.

"You are no relative to me," he said. "I don't care what century you come from."

"But—"

"I am a descendant of Black Hawk," Jim said, "leader of the Sac and Fox Nation. A century ago, he fought a great battle. Five hundred Indians against twelve thousand United States soldiers. The white men captured Black Hawk, took our land, and slaughtered hundreds of our tribe.

Women and children too. I will *never* forget what happened to my people."

At that moment, a voice called from the other end of the construction site.

"Thorpe!" a man yelled. "Slacking off again? You lazy Indian! Get back to work or go home! There are plenty of able-bodied men waiting to take your place."

Jim took his shovel and jammed it hard into the dirt. "I wish we could talk more, but . . ."

"Thorpe!" his boss yelled again.

Bobby and I said good-bye and found a quiet spot off to the side where we could sit down on a couple of cinder blocks. I pulled the new pack out of my pocket again and tore the wrapper off, plucking out one of the cards. I didn't even look to see which player was on the front.

Bobby took my hand without any protest this time. We closed our eyes and I concentrated on going home. Back to Louisville. Back to *my* century.

Soon the tingling sensation started and I breathed a sigh of relief. It was working. The buzzing feeling went up my arms and down my legs. It got stronger and stronger, and then I felt myself disappear.

7

One Mississippi, Two Mississippi . . .

WE LANDED IN A GRASSY FIELD. THAT WAS STRANGE. Usually when I come home, I come *home*. Like, to my bedroom.

"Where are we?" I asked Bobby Fuller, who had tumbled to the ground next to me.

"Sheppard Park," Bobby said. "I play football here sometimes."

The field was perfect for football—flat and rectangular with no bushes or trees in the way. In fact, there were four boys tossing a football around. They looked to be about our age. I didn't know them, but Bobby said a couple of them went to his church.

"Hey Fuller," one of the guys hollered, "you and your friend wanna play some touch? With you two, we can play three-on-three."

"We have school tomorrow," I whispered to Bobby.

"It's getting late."

The truth is, I didn't want to play. Football is not my game. I was never any good at it. Like I said, my hands are small, and I don't like guys chasing me around, knocking me down. I like to stand in a batter's box and take my three swings.

"Sure!" Bobby yelled to the guys. "Lemme see the ball."

Man, I *hate* Bobby Fuller. I felt like walking off and leaving, but I didn't want to look like a wimp.

"I'm no good," I said, following Bobby as he jogged over to join them. "I can't throw a football. Can't catch it either."

"We'll put you on the line," Bobby told me.

We divided into two teams of three guys each. I was on a team with Bobby and this skinny black kid named Reggie.

"You guys kick off," Reggie yelled to the other team, and the three of us dropped back to receive.

"Let me and Reggie handle the ball," Bobby said. "You block."

Fine by me. I didn't want to run with the ball anyway.

One of the kids on the other team kicked off. It was high, end-over-end, and deep. Reggie dropped back to catch it. He took a few steps and lateraled the ball to Bobby. The other team was charging downfield toward us. I got into position to block.

"Go left, Stoshack!" Bobby yelled from behind me.

I did what he told me. I got about ten yards before some guy creamed me from the side. They tagged Bobby right there.

"Okay, okay!" Bobby said, clapping his hands. "First down from here. You okay, Stoshack?"

"Yeah," I said.

I got up slowly. I've been in plenty of collisions playing baseball before, but nothing like this. When you're rounding third and there's a throw coming to the plate, you *know* you're going to crash into the catcher and try to knock the ball loose. You can anticipate it and protect yourself. In football, some guy can come out of nowhere and flatten you.

We huddled up. Bobby and Reggie worked out a play where Reggie was going to run downfield ten yards, then fake left and cut right, where Bobby would hit him with the pass. My job was to hike the ball when Bobby said the word "provolone" and then protect him from the rush.

"Cheddar!" Bobby yelled. "Monterey Jack! Swiss! Provolone!"

I hiked the ball to Bobby. He dropped back.

"One Mississippi . . . two Mississippi . . . three Mississippi . . ." said the guy on the other side of the line.

Reggie ran his pass pattern and Bobby whipped a perfect spiral into his hands. Reggie got tagged right there.

"All right! All right!" Bobby yelled, clapping as he marched upfield. He and Reggie slapped hands.

On the next play, Reggie faked right and went deep.

"He's going long!" one of the guys on the other team yelled desperately.

Bobby threw a long bomb and Reggie caught it right by the tree we had agreed would be the goal line.

Touchdown! Me and Reggie and Bobby high-fived each other.

I had to admit that Bobby could really throw a football. No wonder he gave up baseball.

The guys on the other team were good too. After Reggie kicked off to them, they marched down the field in five or six plays and scored on us to tie it up.

I was getting a little beat up blocking and trying to rush their quarterback, but nothing serious. Hopefully, it wasn't *too* obvious that I didn't know what I was doing.

"Hey, I gotta be home in half an hour," one of the guys on the other team said after they scored.

"Okay, next touchdown wins it," Reggie said, and everyone agreed.

We dropped back to receive the kick. Bobby caught it on one bounce near our goal line. He handed it off to Reggie, who made it to midfield before he got tagged.

"Okay, let's fake them out and win this thing right now," Bobby said to me as we huddled. "After you hike the ball, *you* go out for the pass and Reggie will stay on the line."

"Yeah!" Reggie said. "That's brilliant! Cross 'em up."

"Me?" I said. "Wh—what should I do?"

"Just go deep!" Bobby told me. "They'll be so surprised, they won't know what hit 'em. Okay? Hike the ball on 'mozzarella.'"

I didn't want to do it. But I didn't want to look like a dork, either. We got into position for the play. I wondered what the deal was with Bobby and cheese.

"Muenster!" Bobby called. "American! Mozzarella!"

I hiked the ball to Bobby and took off downfield. Nobody blocked me at the line. The defense was confused because *I* was going out for the pass instead of Reggie. It took them a second or two before they figured out that the guy who normally covered Reggie should cover me instead. By then, I had a ten-yard head start off the line.

As I streaked for the goal line, I turned around to see Bobby chucking the ball long and deep.

It was like slow motion after that. The ball was in a tight spiral, the laces turning clockwise. It was a high, arching pass against the sky. I had the defender beat by about five yards, but he was gaining on me. As the ball was coming down, I reached up with both hands to pull it in.

But somehow, the ball bounced off my hands.

It popped into the air. I tripped and fell, and the guy who was guarding me fell on top of me. I could see the ball was still a few feet off the ground, but I couldn't get up to grab it.

The guy on top of me could, though. He snatched the ball just before it hit the grass and started running upfield with it. Bobby and Reggie took off after him, but it was no use. The guy was really fast, and he ran the whole length of the sideline for a touchdown. His teammates pounded him on the back.

"You are an *idiot*, Stoshack!" Bobby yelled at me. "I put that ball right in your *hands*! How could you drop it? You are useless, man!"

I was filthy, lying in the dirt. There were grass stains on my clothes and bruises all over my body. My jeans were torn at the knee. I was a mess.

Everybody said their good-byes, and Reggie told me the best way to get back to my neighborhood. Bobby just split without a word. I guess he was mad at me for dropping the pass.

I dragged myself home, where my mom was waiting with hugs and kisses.

"What happened to *you*?" she asked. "Did Jim Thorpe beat you up? Where's Bobby?"

"We were playing a little touch football," I said.

"Touch?" she said. "I'd hate to see what you'd look like if you played tackle."

After I took a shower, I looked more presentable. But I felt sort of depressed. Depressed about the football game, and even more depressed because I was still thinking about Jim Thorpe. It wasn't fair.

Here was a guy who was the greatest athlete in the world, and he was digging ditches for a living.

Thorpe reminded me a little of Shoeless Joe Jackson, who played for the Chicago White Sox. He was one of the best hitters ever, but some of his teammates took money from gamblers to lose the World Series on purpose. Jackson was innocent, but he got kicked out of baseball for the rest of his life. That wasn't fair either.

I had done my job. I had arranged for Bobby Fuller to meet Jim Thorpe. That could have been the end of it. We accomplished what Bobby said he wanted to accomplish. We had a little adventure and returned home safely.

But something was gnawing at me. So the next day after school, I did what I usually do when I need to talk to somebody. I rode my bike over to Flip's store.

Flip was signing an autograph for some kid when I came in, but as soon as the kid left, Flip waved me over. He could tell that something was wrong.

"What's eatin' *you?*" Flip asked.

I told him what happened when I went back to 1931 and met Jim Thorpe. Flip knew the whole story of Thorpe losing his Olympic medals. Flip knows just about everything about old-time sports.

"When I was a kid," Flip explained, "the Olympics were for rich folks. It was their exclusive little club for people who didn't have to work to earn a living. They acted like it was beneath a 'gentle-man' to compete for money. The glory should be enough, y'know? So they banned professional athletes from the Olympics. It kept out the riffraff, regular working people. But they made it seem like it was some big 'virtue' to be an amateur."

The more I learned about the situation with Jim Thorpe, the madder I got. Banning professionals from the Olympics was almost like banning African Americans from major-league baseball. As far as I was concerned, all the world records and stats and gold medals didn't mean anything if certain people weren't allowed to compete for them.

"It's just not fair," I said to Flip.

"Yeah," Flip agreed, "but it's like I tell ya, Stosh. Life ain't always fair."

"But maybe I can *fix* it," I whispered, just in case any customers came in. "I could go back and do something to help him. I just need to get an earlier Jim Thorpe card. Will you help me find one?"

Flip sighed.

"Stosh, fuhgetaboutit," he said. "You always think you can fix stuff. But what's done is done. It's history. Nobody remembers Jim Thorpe anymore. It wouldn't make a difference to anybody."

He was probably right. Other than Bobby Fuller, who really cared about Jim Thorpe anyway?

The bell on the door jangled and Flip and I looked up. It was Laverne, Flip's wife.

Flip's *wife*.

I knew what Flip was thinking when Laverne walked in. He knew what I was thinking too.

If it wasn't for me, Flip wouldn't *have* a wife. It's true! When Flip started coaching my Little League team, he wasn't married. But when we went back in time together looking for Satchel Paige, we met this pretty waitress in a restaurant. She fell for Flip big-time. I had to leave the two of them back in 1942. But when I got back from the past, there were Flip and Laverne, an old married couple who were happy and totally in love with each other. And Flip was in the Baseball Hall of Fame.

Time travel is the strangest thing.

One time I asked my science teacher about time travel. He told me it was physically impossible. He said traveling through time would defy Newton's laws of physics, or Einstein's theory of relativity, I don't remember which. But it was against *some* law.

"You can't change history," he told me.

But I knew something that my science teacher didn't know. I can travel through time, and I *can* change history. Maybe I didn't save Shoeless Joe Jackson's career. But I saved the life of my great-uncle Wilbur. And I got Flip a wife. If it wasn't for me, Laverne wouldn't be standing there right now.

"Why are you staring at me?" she asked Flip.

"Because you're so beautiful, honey," Flip said.

"Oh stop it!" she replied, and they started hugging each other.

I knew what I had to do. I had to go back in time

and try to help Jim Thorpe, just like I had helped Flip and Uncle Wilbur. Maybe things would turn out differently. Maybe people *would* remember the name "Jim Thorpe." I could right a wrong. I could change the world in a small way. I had to at least try.

Flip knew it too.

"Okay," he said to me. "I'll help you."

8

Little Pieces of
Cardboard

FLIP VALENTINI KNOWS *EVERYBODY* IN THE WORLD OF
card collecting. These guys are all buddies and
they're constantly swapping and buying each
other's stuff. They even go to conventions so they
can sit around and tell stories about cards
they bought, cards they almost bought, cards they
should have bought, and cards they never should
have sold. Collecting cards is their lives. I'm telling
you, they're obsessed. Who would think that little
pieces of cardboard could be so interesting to somebody?

But I will say one thing: they sure know baseball
cards.

"This is gonna be tough," Flip said as he opened
a big book listing thousands of cards. "Maybe impossible. We gotta find a Thorpe card from before he

was in the Olympics."

Flip told me to put the CLOSED sign on the door so we could work on the problem without being interrupted. When he didn't find anything in the book, he fired up his computer and started cruising baseball card websites.

He poked his stubby fingers around the keyboard, hunt-and-peck style. Flip was pretty computer literate for an old guy. But I guess he never learned how to type.

The first thing we discovered was that Jim Thorpe played for a team called the Rocky Mount Railroaders in the Eastern Carolina League during the summers of 1909 and 1910. That's why his Olympic medals were taken away. If there was a Jim Thorpe card from that league, it would be perfect. I could go back to 1909 and convince him to stop playing baseball, or at least to play under a different name so he wouldn't get caught after the 1912 Olympics.

But Flip checked all his usual web sources, and there was no such card. Semi-pro teams hardly ever printed cards of their players.

The first card we found with Thorpe on it was from 1913, the year after the Olympics. It was his rookie year in the big leagues. Right after his medals were taken away, Jim was signed by the New York Giants. That was long before they moved to San Francisco and became the San Francisco Giants.

Jim was in the front row, first guy on the left.

The 1913 card had a group photo of the Giants team on it. It was put out by Fatima, a cigarette company. There was Jim, sitting in the front row, first guy on the left.

"These go from a couple hundred bucks up to a thousand, depending on the condition," Flip told me as he printed out a copy of the card.

"That's too late," I told Flip. "The Olympics were in 1912."

"Hang on a sec," Flip said. "There's one more possibility . . . AHA! Here's another Thorpe card!"

We read off the screen together:

"From 1909 through 1912, a gum company called Colgan's sold little metal containers with a round card and a piece of mint-flavored gum. They were called Colgan's Chips and sold for five cents."

Bingo! Maybe a Colgan's card would take me back to *before* the summer Olympics. That would be too late to tell Jim not to play ball for the Rocky Mount Railroaders, but at least I could warn him not to enter the Olympics. If he didn't participate in the Olympics, then his life would never be ruined. After all, if you don't win any medals, they can't take them away from you, right?

"That card could work!" I told Flip.

"There's only one problem," he said.

"What?"

"There are only two of 'em."

"Two of them for sale?" I asked.

"No. Two of 'em in the *world*."

So much for *that* idea. It didn't look like I was going to visit Jim Thorpe again anytime soon.

The next day I went for my weekly visit with my dad, who lives in an assisted-living development in Louisville. A few years after my parents split up, Dad got into a bad car crash and he's been in a wheelchair ever since. He can't work and doesn't get around very well.

My dad used to be a *huge* baseball fan. He's the one who taught me how to play and got me interested in collecting cards. But when the news came out that a lot of players were taking steroids, my dad lost interest in the game. He said if guys took drugs to build up their muscles and then they hit 70 home runs in a season, it made all the statistics of baseball history meaningless. You can't compare the stats of a guy who was juiced with those of a guy who wasn't.

Since baseball was pretty much my dad's life, he sort of lost interest in life at the same time. He was depressed. It wasn't much fun to go visit him. But I had to because, well, he's my dad.

Usually, we'd talk about the old days. That seemed to cheer him up.

"Do you know anything about Jim Thorpe?" I asked him.

"The guy from the Olympics?" Dad replied. "Sure. You thinkin' of going to visit him?"

"I already did," I said, "but I was too late. I'm thinking of going back and talking to him before the Olympics."

"Not a bad idea," Dad said. "Jim Thorpe totally blew it."

"Huh?"

"After he won the Olympics, Thorpe was sitting on a gold mine," my dad told me. "He could've made millions, even without any medals. You know what they say: Everybody is famous for 15 minutes. Well, Thorpe was the most famous man in the world. He could have cashed in big-time—movies, ads, exhibitions. He could have toured the world and raked it in."

"So why didn't he?"

"Because he was stupid," Dad said. "You know what he did instead of cashing in on his Olympic fame? He went back to college and played football. For *free*. How dumb was that? A few months later, nobody cared about him anymore. I'm telling you, money makes the world go 'round. Some people know how to make it, and some people don't."

I looked around my dad's tiny apartment. Everything was old or faded or broken. This was a man who didn't know how to make money.

I pulled out the picture of the New York Giants card that Flip had printed for me and showed it to my dad.

"That's *right*!" he said. "Thorpe played for the New York Giants. With Christy Mathewson! With John McGraw! What a team! They *owned* New York back then. They owned baseball! Oh, you gotta go just to meet those guys!"

For the first time in a long while, I saw a little spark in Dad's eyes. He was excited.

"Remember the time we saw Babe Ruth in the 1932 World Series?" I asked.

That was one of the best times Dad and I ever had. Ruth hit his famous "called shot" home run in that Series. He pointed to the centerfield wall and then hit the next pitch over it. Or that's the legend, anyway. Nobody knew for sure whether or not Ruth *really* called his shot. But we knew exactly when and where he was going to hit it, so Dad and I decided to go back and see with our own eyes. It's a long story.

"That was before I got hurt," Dad said, shifting his weight in his wheelchair.

I felt bad. There wasn't a whole lot my dad could do anymore.

"I probably won't see any baseball players," I told Dad. "If I'm lucky, I'll get to Jim Thorpe before he gets into the majors."

"Well, do me a favor, will you?" Dad asked. "If you happen to meet John McGraw, get him to sign something for me. I know a guy who collects nothing but McGraw memorabilia. This guy is nuts. He'll pay *anything* for signed McGraw stuff."

That old fire flickered in my dad's eyes again. It made him look younger.

"I'll try, Dad," I said.

A couple of days later, when I got home from school, Flip Valentini was knocking on the front door.

"I got somethin' for you," he said.

"Don't tell me," I said. "You tracked down one of the two guys in the world who owns the Colgan's Jim Thorpe card?"

"How'd you know?" Flip asked.

"I was joking!" I said. "You mean, you really got it?"

Flip took an envelope out of his jacket pocket and pulled out the Colgan's card, which was in a plastic sleeve.

"The owner is *very* protective," Flip said. "He's

never even tried to sell this card at an auction."

"Wow." I marveled, looking at it. "How much is it worth?"

"Lemme put it this way," Flip said as he handed me the card. "You lose this, and you owe me 50,000 bucks."

9

Do Your Own Thing

BOBBY FULLER'S LOCKER IS MILES AWAY FROM MY LOCKER. But I kept going there all morning between classes, hoping to see him. After my third or fourth try, I figured that Bobby probably never even goes to his locker. If you don't do your schoolwork and you fail all your classes, what do you need a locker for anyway?

But finally, toward the end of lunch period, I spotted Bobby at his locker. He was laughing with a few of his pre-juvenile-delinquent friends.

Some kids, like me, are into sports. Some kids are into music or art. Bobby and his friends, I'm guessing, are into setting off homemade fireworks and pulling the wings off insects.

As soon as I got within ten feet, Bobby and his friends stopped laughing. I'm sure they were planning something that was illegal, or should be.

"What are you lookin' at, choirboy?" this guy wearing a Metallica T-shirt asked.

I can't sing and I've never been in a choir. I guess he was trying to suggest that I was one of those kids who follow the rules and don't get into trouble all the time. As if that was a *bad* thing.

The first words that popped into my mind were, *Just looking at some garbage*. But I decided to keep my mouth shut.

"I asked you, What are you lookin' at?" the kid repeated.

"Nothing," I replied.

Metallica Boy stepped right up in my face.

"You tryin' to say I'm nothin'?"

I took a quick look around. I could probably take the kid, but my school has a zero-tolerance policy about fighting. It wasn't worth getting suspended just to see this guy with a bloody nose.

"Knock it off, Duane," Bobby said. "He ain't bothering nobody."

"What are *you*?" Duane asked Bobby. "One of *them*?"

"Let's leave these two alone," one of the other guys said. "They probably want to do their homework together."

Bobby's idiot friends laughed as if that was funny and walked away.

"So long, Bobby," Duane said as they left. "I hope you two get straight As."

What a bunch of jerks.

"Okay, Stoshack," Bobby said when his friends were gone. "What do you want?"

"I have something to show you," I told him.

I swung off my backpack and took out the Colgan's Jim Thorpe card. I kept it in the plastic sleeve, partly to protect it and partly to prevent me from sending myself back in time by accident.

"What's this?" Bobby asked as he slipped the card out of its sleeve. "This ain't no baseball card."

"It'll work," I said. "Be *careful* with it!"

Bobby looked at me with his evil grin. Then he pinched the card and held it like he was going to rip it in half.

"No, *don't*!" I screamed.

Suddenly the hall was silent. Everybody was looking at me.

Bobby laughed. "Relax. I wasn't gonna rip it," he said. "I was just goofing on you."

"It's worth 50,000 bucks!" I whispered. "There are only two of them in the *world*!"

"Look, Stoshack," Bobby said as he slipped the card back into its sleeve. "I already met Jim Thorpe. The guy turned out to be a loser. Give it a rest."

"But he's your great-grandfather!" I said.

"So what?" said Bobby. "He was a jerk. He dissed me. Nobody treats me like that. I hate him."

The bell was about to ring. Lunch period was almost over. But I wasn't ready to give up.

"Think about it," I said to Bobby. "This card was printed sometime between 1909 and 1912. I read it on the Internet. The Olympics were in 1912. If we can get to Jim *before* the Olympics, we can convince him not to compete. If he's not in the Olympics, he won't win the medals. And if he doesn't win the medals, they can't take them away from him."

Bobby thought it over. I have to give him credit for that.

"But if he doesn't win the medals," he said, "Jim Thorpe will be a nobody."

I couldn't argue with that, and I had to admit he had a point. You can't be infamous if you're not famous. Which is worse—to be famous for doing something wrong, or to be a nobody your whole life?

I wasn't sure. But my gut told me that, at least in this case, doing something was better than doing nothing.

"Don't you ever feel like something is just the right thing to do?" I asked Bobby. "I mean, this is your chance to right a serious wrong. Not many people ever have the chance to do that in their whole lives."

The bell rang. I had to get to math.

"You can't change me, Stoshack," Bobby said. "You're not gonna turn me into a Goody Two-shoes do-gooder like you. I'm gonna do my own thing."

"Fine," I said, turning on my heel. "Do your own thing."

I don't need Bobby Fuller, I thought to myself as I walked down the hall to class. Bringing him along only makes things more complicated anyway. I'll just do it on my own. He can do his thing and I'll do mine.

Every time I go back in time, Mom and Uncle Wilbur act like they're sending me off to sleepaway camp. Mom was running around putting snacks, Band-Aids, an umbrella, and other stuff in a suitcase for me to take. No *way* was I taking a suitcase with me to 1912.

Uncle Wilbur dug up some of his old clothes, which he saved from back when he was my age. He grew up *after* 1912, but he insisted that his clothes would still look current because men's fashions don't change that much from year to year. He pulled out a white button-down shirt, suspenders, a brown hat with a tiny little brim, and a pair of gray pants that stopped at knee level. Then he gave me a pair of socks that went all the way up to the bottom of the pants. They looked ridiculous, but I put the stuff on anyway.

"You look like a million bucks," Uncle Wilbur told me.

Besides the baseball card, there was only one thing I wanted to bring along with me—the newspaper article I had copied at the library about Jim losing his medals. If I could prove to him that competing in the Olympics would ruin his life, it might help him to make up his mind.

Everything was ready. I patted my pocket to make sure I had the Colgan's card and a new pack of cards to bring me back home. Uncle Wilbur wished me good luck and went upstairs to bed. Mom gave me a hug and told me to be careful (for the hundredth time). I sat on the couch and got myself ready.

That's when the doorbell rang. Mom went to get it so I wouldn't have to explain why I was dressed so oddly. I was more than a little surprised when she came back into the living room with Bobby Fuller.

"What are *you* doing here?" I asked.

"Joey, is that any way to talk to your friend?" Mom said.

"Mom!" I shouted, shooing her upstairs.

"I changed my mind," Bobby told me. "I want to go too."

Maybe it would be *good* if Bobby came along, I tried to convince myself. If I got into a jam, he might be able to bail me out. After all, he *did* save my life when that wrecking ball almost creamed me the first time.

"Okay, put these duds on," I told Bobby.

"Are you kidding me?" Bobby said. "Suspenders are for clowns. You look like you should be in the circus, Stoshack."

"You want to blend in when we get there, don't you?" I told him. "You don't want to look like some freak."

"All right, all right," Bobby agreed. "But I gotta bring my backpack with me."

"What do you have in there, anyway?" I asked.

"I *told* you, my meds," he replied. "That, and my iPod."

"You're bringing an iPod?!"

I couldn't believe it. If the people in 1912 saw an iPod, they'd probably spaz out, call the cops, and have us thrown in jail.

"A man's gotta have his tunes," Bobby explained.

I could have argued. You can argue about anything. But then you find yourself arguing all the time. If he wanted to bring an iPod with him, that was his business.

Bobby went into the bathroom and came out wearing Uncle Wilbur's clothes. They were a little small on him, but he didn't look that bad. He actually looked more like a regular kid.

We sat on the couch. I took a few deep breaths to relax, and held out my right hand. This time, Bobby took it without complaining.

"Ready?" I asked.

"Let's blow this pop stand," he said.

I dipped my other hand in my pocket and took out the Colgan's card. I needed to tap the plastic sleeve against the coffee table to make the card slip out.

The tingling sensation didn't come immediately. Sometimes it takes a while. I have to get in the mood, relax, and think about where I'm going. Early 1912, I hoped. Someplace, I wasn't sure where. Somewhere in the general vicinity of Jim Thorpe. I knew that much. We could end up on an Indian reservation—or in Stockholm, Sweden, where the Olympics took place. Or anywhere. That was part of the mystery. I just hoped Bobby Fuller wouldn't mess things up for me. It was a big risk, taking him along. I'd have to be very careful.

"It's happening," Bobby whispered. "I can feel it."

He was right. I had been thinking so much that I didn't even notice my fingers were starting to tingle.

"Is everything gonna be in black-and-white?" Bobby whispered.

"*Shhhhhh!*" I said. "No."

The buzzy feeling moved up my arm quickly. Soon it washed across me like a crowd doing the wave at a game and my whole body was vibrating. I wished I could bottle that feeling, because there's nothing like it in the world.

Then I started to feel the atoms that make up my very existence disappear one by one, like when you pop bubble wrap until there are no pops left. My body was vanishing from the present and moving through space and time to another era.

We were gone.

10

The Truth About
Bobby Fuller

WHEN I OPENED MY EYES, THE FIRST THING I SAW WAS A ballpark. But I wasn't *in* the ballpark. I was up on a big, rocky hill overlooking it. Part of the field was visible, but most of it was blocked by the stands.

I didn't recognize the place. It was in the shape of a big horseshoe. There were apartment buildings all around. It was in the middle of a big city, that was for sure.

New York? Maybe. There were wooden water towers on the roofs of buildings around the park. But it wasn't Yankee Stadium. I had been there. It couldn't be Shea Stadium either. That wasn't built until the 1960s.

There was a chill in the air. It felt like early spring, maybe March or April. The beginning of baseball season. The sun was high in the sky. It must be around noon, I figured.

Suddenly I remembered Bobby Fuller was with me. I wheeled around and there he was, lying on the grass. He was asleep, snoring. Jet lag, I guess. Going back a century in time must have knocked the wind out of him. Me, I'm used to it.

Bobby's backpack was on the ground, and the zipper was open a couple of inches. He seemed so protective about his stuff. What did he have in there anyway? I wasn't sure if it would be an invasion of Bobby's privacy to peek inside. But as long as he was taking a snooze, there was no harm in poking around a little. I opened the zipper a few more inches and looked inside.

His iPod was on top, with the earbuds wrapped around it. Underneath were two small medicine bottles. They didn't have labels on them, but I could see there was liquid inside.

Hmm, that was odd. I always thought kids with ADD took their medicine in the form of pills.

I dug a little deeper, and that's when I found something that blew my mind—a syringe. A hypodermic needle. One of those things doctors use to give you a shot.

Why would a kid have a syringe? Couldn't Bobby just take his medicine with a spoon? I know lots of kids with ADD and none of them have to inject themselves.

There was only one logical explanation. I hated to think it was true, but it was obvious.

Bobby Fuller was a junkie!

I had heard that some kids my age were addicted to drugs, but I'd never met anyone who used them. Maybe I was wrong. Maybe I just didn't *know* they were using drugs.

This was *horrible*. I looked at the bottles again. In school one time they showed us a movie about drugs, and they said junkies inject heroin into themselves with needles.

Suddenly, I felt a little differently about Bobby Fuller. All these years I'd hated him for the mean things he had done to me. Maybe I should have pitied him. Maybe being addicted to heroin was what messed him up so much. Maybe he couldn't control himself. This explained a lot.

I looked at Bobby's arms to see if there were any needle marks on them. He didn't have any, but I know that junkies can be very clever. They know how to shoot themselves up in different parts of their body without leaving marks. That was in the movie too.

My first impulse was to throw the syringe and bottles away so Bobby couldn't use them. But no, that would be wrong. If he's addicted to the stuff, who knows what might happen if he couldn't get it? I decided to play it cool and not say a word. Pretend I didn't know Bobby was a drug addict. When we got back home, I'd ask my mom what I could do to get Bobby some help. She's a nurse and knows about treatment programs for people who have substance-abuse problems.

"Uuuuuuuh!" Bobby mumbled, stretching out his arms.

Quickly, I jammed the stuff into his backpack and zipped it closed.

"Are you okay, man?" I asked Bobby. "Do you need to be by yourself for a while?"

"Where are we?" Bobby asked.

"I'm not sure," I said, "but something tells me Jim Thorpe is around here somewhere."

The hill we were standing on looked like it would be a good place to watch a ball game without paying admission. You couldn't see the whole field, but you could see leftfield, centerfield, and the area around second base. In fact, there were a few people with picnic baskets spreading out blankets and setting up lawn chairs. They were dressed a lot like us in their old-fashioned clothes.

Bobby and I walked over to an older couple, who were fanning themselves and eating.

"Excuse me," I said. "Where are we?"

"Whaddaya mean, where are we?" the man snapped. "You dumb or somethin'?"

"Perhaps they're from out of town, dear," the lady said.

"Yes," I explained, "we're from Louisville, Kentucky."

"Welcome to New York," the lady said, shaking our hands. "This is Coogan's Bluff."

I'd never heard of Coogan's Bluff. Neither had Bobby, by the look on his face.

"Told you they were dumb," her husband remarked.

"It's right outside the Polo Grounds." The lady pointed to the field. "You know, where the Giants play."

"Is there a game today?" I asked.

"Oh, yes!" the lady replied.

"The Giants?" Bobby said. "The Giants play in San Francisco. And you say *we're* dumb!"

"Who ya callin' dumb?" the man said, jumping to his feet and putting up his dukes.

I pulled Bobby aside and whispered that the Giants *used* to play in New York. They moved to San Francisco in the late 1950s, the same time the Brooklyn Dodgers moved to Los Angeles.

"Please excuse my friend," I told the couple. "He's, uh . . . learning disabled."

"He's *what*?" said the guy. "I should disable his *face*! What's that you got? A fancy purse?"

"It's a backpack," Bobby said.

"Looks like a purse to me."

Bobby was itching to fight the guy, but I pulled him away. We crossed the bluff and started walking down a long staircase toward the ballpark, passing two signs marking the intersection of 157th Street and Eighth Avenue. The streets were mostly empty. There were a few cars parked on the block, those old-time cars you see in silent movies.

"Why do they call it the Polo Grounds?" Bobby asked me.

"I don't know," I replied. "Maybe they used to play polo here."

There was a garbage can on the corner. I reached into it.

"Stoshack, what are you doing?" Bobby shouted. "Don't be a pig, man! You don't know what's in there. That's disgusting!"

"I'm looking for a newspaper," I explained, and soon I found one.

NEW YORK, SATURDAY, FEBRUARY 1, 1913. — TWENTY-FOUR PAGES

Oh, no! It was 1913! I had read on a website that the Colgan's cards were printed from 1909 to 1912. It must have been wrong! I let out a few well-chosen curse words and stamped my foot. That is the *last* time I will ever trust any fact I read on the Internet.

"1913!" Bobby yelled. "Stoshack, we're too late! You screwed up again! What happened? I thought you said that card was from 1912."

"I thought it *was*," I said. "The website had it wrong. Maybe it was printed in 1913. I don't know. I told you, time travel isn't an exact science."

"This sucks, man!" Bobby moaned. "You're hopeless, Stoshack. What are we wasting our time for? Let's get outta here."

I ignored him. I didn't travel a century back in time just to turn around and go home as if I remembered I had left the water running. I scanned the headlines in the paper until something caught my eye:

THORPE IS TO PLAY BALL WITH GIANTS

Famous Indian Athlete Accepts McGraw's Terms Over the Telephone.

WILL GET AT LEAST $5,000

Dethroned World's Champion Coming to New York To-day to Sign Contract — Western Clubs Outbid.

" Jim " Thorpe, the Carlisle Indian, who was crowned the world's greatest athlete at the Olympic games at Stockholm last July and has been stripped of his amateur achievements because he has confessed to playing professional baseball three years ago in the South was made a member of the New York Giants yesterday by Manager John J. McGraw. Thorpe accepted the terms of the New York club over the long-distance telephone and will report to Manager McGraw at the club office in the Fifth Avenue Building at 2 o'clock this afternoon to sign his contract.

Five days after his Olympic medals were taken away, Jim Thorpe signed to play baseball.

"Look at this," I told Bobby.

The article went on to say that the Giants signed

Jim hoping he would bring them a championship. They had lost the last two World Series. In 1911 they were beaten by the Philadelphia A's and in 1912 the Boston Red Sox beat them. I didn't know how old the newspaper was. It could have been in the trash for a while.

"The Red Sox?" Bobby said, reading over my shoulder. "I thought they were cursed for like 80 years after they sold Babe Ruth to the Yankees."

"This is *before* they sold Ruth," I told Bobby. "This is even before they *signed* Ruth. It's 1913. Babe Ruth didn't start playing until 1914."

"Well, excuse me, Mr. Baseball," Bobby cracked.

We walked around the perimeter of the ballpark. The place looked like it was deserted. A sign said that game time was at 3:30. Admission was 25 cents for bleacher seats and 50 cents for box seats. Man, stuff was cheap in 1913.

The only problem was, I didn't have *any* money. There was no way for us to get inside.

"Where's that wad of cash you wanted to pay me?" I asked Bobby.

"I left it at home," he said.

"Lot of good it'll do us there."

It occurred to me that Bobby's money wouldn't do us any good even if we had it. Money has changed a lot since 1913. If we tried to use bills from the twenty-first century, we'd be arrested for counterfeiting. It almost happened to me before.

"I guess we're gonna have to panhandle or

something," I said.

"Panhandle?" Bobby said. "Are you kidding me, Stoshack? I'm not begging for money."

"Then how do *you* suggest we get inside?" I asked. "Rob somebody?"

"Haven't you ever snuck in anywhere without paying?" Bobby asked, as if that was a normal thing to do.

"No," I told him. I've never cheated on a test or beat anyone up or shoplifted or took drugs either—all things that Bobby probably did regularly.

"You've got a lot to learn, Stoshack," Bobby said. "Follow me."

We continued walking around the outside of the Polo Grounds, trying to open every door we passed. They were all locked. Bobby wanted to hop over a brick wall near the outfield fence, but it was too high and there was no place to dig a toe in to climb up.

Finally we came to a window. It was about four feet off the ground and Bobby was able to push it open. He had me give him a boost so he could get his body inside.

"Isn't this breaking and entering?" I asked.

"We didn't break anything," Bobby assured me. "We're just entering. And I don't see any sign that says you can't."

Once he was inside, he pulled me through the window too. It was an office, with one of those roll-top desks and an old-time typewriter on it.

"Come on," Bobby said, "Let's look around."

He opened the door and led me into a dark tunnel as if he knew where he was going. The tunnel twisted around and it looked like it was heading nowhere until Bobby pushed open a door. Sunlight flooded the hallway, and after we walked through the door we were standing in—

the outfield!

I couldn't believe it. We were standing in the outfield of the legendary Polo Grounds! It was one of the most famous ballparks in history. The Giants played there for decades. The Yankees played there when Yankee Stadium was under construction. The Mets played there while they were waiting for Shea Stadium to be finished.

I couldn't resist running across the grass and diving for an imaginary fly ball. What a catch! Bobby ran over to second base and slid into it, kicking up a spray of dirt. We ran around like we were crazy. This place was the coolest. And we had the whole field to ourselves.

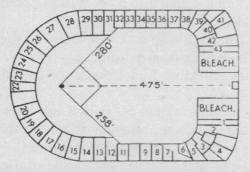

The Polo Grounds had a really strange shape.

The Polo Grounds was like no other ballpark I'd ever seen. The leftfield and rightfield lines weren't marked, but they were really short, less than 300 feet. Centerfield went on *forever*. You had to hit a ball *real* hard to get it over the fence in straightaway center.

The outfield walls were plastered with ads for Bromo-Seltzer, Lifebuoy soap, Chesterfield cigarettes, and Coca-Cola. They had one of those old scoreboards with holes in it where the numbers would be put up. And there were no lights towering over the field. The first night game wouldn't be played until the 1930s.

I couldn't get over the fact that I was in the same place where Bobby Thomson would hit "the shot heard 'round the world" to win the 1951 pennant. I was in the place where Willie Mays would make his famous over-the-shoulder catch in the 1954 World Series.

In the twenty-first century, the Polo Grounds doesn't even exist anymore. The ballpark was demolished a long time ago, after the Giants moved to San Francisco. But here I was, standing in its high grass like I owned the place.

"Hey!" a voice suddenly thundered. "How'd you kids get in here?"

That's when somebody grabbed me roughly by the shoulder.

11

It Ain't Cheatin'
If Ya Don't Get Caught

"DID YOU GUTTERSNIPES HOP THE FENCE?"

I turned around to face the man who had grabbed me. He was a huge guy with a big handlebar mustache. On his shirt was embroidered the name MURPHY.

"*Uhhhh,*" I mumbled helplessly.

"We're here to see Jim Thorpe," Bobby said.

"Well, he ain't here," Murphy growled. "The players don't show up till one o'clock. While you're waitin', you two can help me with the groundskeeping."

"*Groundskeeping?*" Bobby said. "Forget it. I've got better things to do."

"Like rotting in juvenile jail?" Murphy asked, as he tightened his grip on our shoulders. "Trespassing is against the law, y'know."

"What do we have to do?" Bobby asked glumly.

Murphy didn't waste any time before putting us to work. First, he showed us how to slope the dirt to one side on the foul lines from home plate to first and third. I couldn't figure out why he would bother sloping them, until he told us that the Giants were really good bunters. Every day he sloped the foul lines so their bunts would be more likely to roll into fair territory instead of going foul. It never would have occurred to me that anyone would even think of doing that. I thought groundskeepers just kept the grass green and the dirt smooth. I thought the idea was to *level* the playing field, not tilt it.

After we finished that job, Murphy gave each of us a bar of soap. I figured he wanted us to wash the dirt off our hands, but he told us to chop the soap up into little pieces with a knife. Then we had to mix the soap in with the dirt around the pitcher's mound. It didn't make any sense to me. But Murphy told us that when opposing pitchers picked up the dirt and rubbed it on their hands, the soap would make their fingers slippery and they'd have trouble throwing the ball over the plate.

"They can't grip it, y'see," Murphy said. "Next, the outfield grass."

"Do you want us to mow it?" I asked.

"Heck, no," Murphy said, taking three baseballs out of a bag. "We keep the grass high on purpose. I want you to go out there and hide a baseball in left-field, centerfield, and rightfield."

"Why?" I asked.

"Stoshack, it's *obvious*," Bobby chimed in. "When the Giants' outfielders can't reach a long drive, they can just pick up one of the balls hidden in the high grass and throw the guy out."

"Now yer usin' yer noodle!" Murphy said as he threw his arm around Bobby's shoulder. "This is my kind of boy!"

"But isn't all this stuff cheating?" I asked.

"It ain't cheatin' if ya don't get caught," Murphy told me.

We had been working for over an hour and I was tired, but Murphy wasn't quite done with us yet. He led us to a cart full of empty barrels under the grandstand and instructed us to roll it over near the Giants' locker room. I wasn't even going to ask why, but Murphy told us that John McGraw, the Giants' manager, is superstitious. He thinks a cart full of barrels brings good luck. So Murphy always makes sure to have a cart full of barrels outside the locker room.

"That's ridiculous," I mumbled, but Bobby and I did what he said.

Finally, we were finished with Murphy's chores. He took two dimes out of his pocket and gave one to each of us.

"Good job, boys," he said. "Just drag those bags of dirty uniforms into the locker room and you can go enjoy the game."

I pushed open the locker-room door and was surprised to see that there were players in there. Guys were lounging around, reading letters, eating, putting on their uniforms, smoking cigarettes, and talking with each other. One guy was rubbing a rabbit's foot. Another was spitting tobacco juice into a metal bowl on the floor. I didn't see anyone who looked like Jim Thorpe. All I could do was stare for a moment.

"Be cool," I whispered to Bobby. "Act like you belong. Don't go asking for autographs."

"Don't tell *me* what to do," he replied. "I'm no dork. Where's Jim Thorpe?"

"He's gotta be around here someplace."

Bobby marched in and started picking up towels and garbage off the floor, as if he was the clubhouse attendant. I did the same, being careful not to make eye contact with any of the players. Maybe if we looked busy, they wouldn't kick us out.

The locker room was old, or maybe it just looked old-fashioned. There were exposed pipes snaking across the ceiling. Everything was made of wood instead of metal or plastic. But for all I knew, this place was state-of-the-art in 1913.

The players' uniforms, I noticed, were really baggy and completely blank on the back. It wasn't until the 1920s that ballplayers had numbers. Names on the jerseys came even later.

Fortunately for us, the players' names were printed on tape above each of the lockers: Fred Merkle. Larry Doyle. Buck Herzog. Red Murray. Josh Devore. Fred Snodgrass. I had heard some of these names before and seen them on old baseball cards.

Most of the Giants were in the same set as the famous Honus Wagner T-206 card.

Finally I found Jim Thorpe's locker, but it was empty. Maybe he was late. Maybe he was sick.

Off in the far corner, some players were crowded around a big table with a bunch of checkerboards on it. One guy in the middle of the group stood out because he was still in his street clothes. He was taller than the others, with bright blue eyes and wavy blond hair that was parted perfectly, like he had used a ruler. He didn't look like a baseball player. He looked like a movie star. This guy I recognized.

"That's Matty!" I whispered to Bobby.

"Matty who?"

"Christy Mathewson!" I told him.

"A *guy* named Christy?"

Matty looked more like a movie star than a baseball player.

I told Bobby that Matty was one of the greatest pitchers in baseball history. In four different seasons, he won 30 games or more. Not 20. *30!* One year he won 37 games.

The players were setting up checkers on six

checkerboards around Matty.

"Ready, gentlemen?" Matty asked.

"This time at least one of us is gonna whup you for sure, Matty," one of them said.

"I'll believe that when I see it."

It was incredible. Matty was going to play six games of checkers at the same time! That was amazing enough. But then he did something even *more* amazing. He took a handkerchief out of his pocket and wrapped it over his eyes!

"Or I'll believe it when I *don't* see it," Matty added.

Oh man, this guy must be one great checkers player. He was playing six guys at the same time, and he was playing them *blindfolded*.

This I had to see. Bobby, however, wasn't as impressed.

"I'm gonna go look for Jim," he said.

Yeah, sure. I remembered the syringe and bottles in Bobby's backpack. He was probably going to find a private place where he could inject himself. I let him go.

It was fascinating to watch Matty play checkers. He must have imagined each board in his head, then made a move, went on to the next board for another move, and so on. Somehow, he was able to keep all six games straight.

I could have watched all day, but suddenly there was a commotion at the other end of the locker room. I stood on a bench to see what was going on.

Two guys were stripped to the waist, wrestling on the floor.

One of them was a big, fat guy. He had to be at least 250 pounds. It should have been no contest, but the smaller guy was quicker and more agile. Nobody broke up the fight. Instead, the players gathered around to watch. So did I.

"Tesreau! Tesreau! Tesreau!" chanted some of the guys.

The other guys chanted, "Thorpe! Thorpe! Thorpe! Thorpe!"

So *that* was Jim Thorpe! It was hard to get a good look at him, because he was moving like a tornado around the fat guy they called Tesreau—grabbing, pulling, grunting, and trying to get into a position where he would have the advantage.

"Take him down, Jimmy!" somebody yelled.

"Sit on him, Jeff!" yelled somebody else.

Where was Bobby? I wondered. *He would want to see this.*

Soon Tesreau was breathing heavily and Jim began to get the upper hand. He moved behind the bigger man, crossing one leg over Tesreau's leg. Then he yanked one of Tesreau's arms over his own head and twisted the other one behind his back.

"I call this the Armbreaker," Jim grunted.

"No! Don't!" moaned Tesreau. "That's my pitching arm!"

"KNOCK IT OFF!" a voice bellowed from behind a door at the other end of the locker room. It said

MANAGER'S OFFICE on it.

The door swung open and slammed against the wall with a crash. Suddenly, everybody stopped what they were doing, like they were playing a game of freeze tag.

Total silence.

12

The Little Napoleon

BOBBY FULLER CAME BACK JUST IN TIME TO SEE THE GUY storm out of his office. It had to be John McGraw, the manager of the Giants. I remembered my dad asking if I could bring home something signed by McGraw. But this sure wasn't the time to ask for an autograph.

"What the hell is going on in here?" McGraw hollered.

John McGraw was a short guy, on the heavy side. "The Little Napoleon," they used to call him. He had small, intense eyes. But he sure had a big mouth. McGraw didn't look that old, but his hair was white. He looked like one of those guys who gets old before his time.

At the sound of McGraw's high-pitched voice, Jim Thorpe and the guy he was wrestling let go of each other.

**Sometimes they called McGraw "The Little Napoleon."
Sometimes they called him "Muggsy."**

"That'll cost you a hundred bucks, Thorpe!" McGraw said as he stormed across the locker room. "How many times do I have to tell you? No boozing! No smoking! No card playing! And *no* wrestling!"

"It's not his fault, Mr. McGraw," said Tesreau. "I challenged him, sir."

"Nobody asked you! And you should be ashamed of yourself, letting a man half your size beat you."

The players slunk off to their lockers. Finally I could get a good look at Jim Thorpe. He was much younger, but I still recognized him from when I saw him in 1931. His chest was even more muscular now. He could have been one of those ripped bodybuilders you see on muscle magazine covers.

But I couldn't take my eyes off McGraw. I don't know if he was always so mean or if he just happened to be in a bad mood. But he looked like he

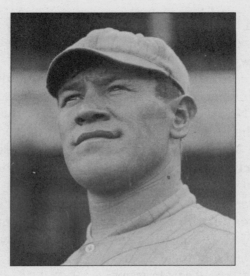

**Jim didn't look like the Indians
I'd seen in movies and on TV.**

hated everybody. There was fire in his eyes.

I was sure McGraw was going to kick me and Bobby out of the locker room. We had no business being in there. I tried to make myself look small, fade into the woodwork. But I didn't have to bother. McGraw seemed intent on giving his players a hard time. They cowered in fear as he stalked around the locker room, looking them over like a general inspecting his troops. He stopped in front of one guy and ripped a cigarette out of his mouth.

"Cigarettes line the guideposts on the path to baseball oblivion!" said McGraw.

"Aw, heck, Skip," the guy said. "I can lick any

team in the league."

"Marquard, you couldn't lick a *stamp*!" spat McGraw. "That'll cost you 50 bucks."

What a jerk. He walked around, insulting and fining just about everybody in the room except for Matty. Nobody argued with John McGraw. Nobody talked back. They all looked like they were terrified.

"Mr. McGraw?" Jim Thorpe asked quietly.

"What?" the manager said, spinning around to see who would dare speak to him.

"I was just wondering if I could get some playing time today. All I've been doing is pinch running and pinch hitting. I really need to get some swings and play every day to—"

"NO!" shouted McGraw.

"Well, why not?"

Everybody turned to look at Jim, as if they couldn't believe he had the nerve to question the judgment of the great John McGraw.

"I brought you here to put fannies in the seats, Thorpe," McGraw fumed. "You were the *Olympic champion*. Everybody was supposed to come out to the Polo Grounds to see *the greatest athlete in the world*. So how come our attendance is down this year, Thorpe?"

"With all due respect, sir," Jim said, "nobody comes to see me because you don't play me."

Somebody gasped. It was as quiet as a tomb.

"I'm not your babysitter! I'm trying to win the pennant!" McGraw thundered. "Why should I play you? You stink!"

"How would you know if you never play me?" Jim muttered under his breath.

A few more guys gasped.

"What did you say?" barked McGraw, getting right in Jim's face.

"Nothin'."

"You are the highest-paid rookie in baseball *history*, Thorpe!" McGraw yelled. "We're paying you *6,000 dollars a year*! And you can't hit a curveball! Matty only gets 9,000, and he's won 300 games for this team. How many did *you* win?"

Bobby and I glanced at each other. 6,000 dollars a year? 9,000? The average salary in our time is about a *million* dollars a year.

"Then release me," Jim argued.

"I'd release you in a heartbeat if you didn't have a three-year contract," McGraw snapped back.

"Then trade me, or send me down to the minors," Jim said. "Some other manager will give me a chance."

"*Nobody* wants you, Thorpe!" McGraw said bitterly. "You can throw a javelin far and you can jump high. Well, that won't cut it in baseball. You gotta use your *head*."

"I *do* use my head," Jim insisted.

"Oh yeah?" McGraw hollered. "Tell me, Thorpe, the count is two and one. There are two outs. Bottom of the sixth. Runners at first and third. We're down by two runs. What do you do? Do you start the runners with the pitch? Straight steal? Double steal? Swing away? Take a pitch? Pinch hit?"

"Bunt," Jim said after thinking it over for a moment.

"NO!" McGraw yelled. "Bunt with two outs? What kind of a bonehead are you? Baseball requires intelligence, and you ain't got it."

"Just give me a *chance!*" Jim pleaded, raising his voice a little. "I've only played a little semi-pro ball. I never even *saw* a good curveball until a couple of—"

"Don't give me your sob story," McGraw snapped. "When I was twelve, my mother, sister, and two of my brothers dropped dead from diphtheria. My wife, Minnie, bless her soul, died when she was twenty-two. You don't see me whining, you dumb redskin."

At that, Jim exploded and went to grab McGraw by the throat. But four of the Giants jumped on him and held him back.

"Go ahead, get angry!" McGraw yelled at him. "That's exactly what you need, Thorpe! I know how to handle scoundrels like you! I've dealt with a hundred of 'em. I can control any man."

Jim was still steaming, but he had calmed down enough so the other players relaxed their grip on him.

I wasn't sure if McGraw was a total jerk or a master psychologist. From watching my own team, I know that some kids play better when Flip tells them how good they are, while other kids play better when they get yelled at. Me, I need a little kick in the pants every once in a while to get me motivated. But John McGraw was really going psycho on Jim.

McGraw finally backed away, and it almost looked like the hint of a smile flashed across his face.

"Boys," he said, "I just signed a new outfielder. I want you to meet him."

McGraw went back into his office and came out with a stocky guy with dark skin. In fact, his skin was so dark that he looked African American to me. But I knew that was impossible. Black players were barred from playing professional baseball until Jackie Robinson broke the color barrier in 1947.

"Afternoon, gents," the guy said, giving a little wave.

"This is Chief Tokahoma," McGraw announced, glancing in Jim's direction. "He's a full-blooded Cherokee. The Chief is gonna take us all the way to the Series this year. It's about time I found an Indian who can play this game."

"But Mr. McGraw, I ain't no Indian," Chief Tokahoma said. "I'm a Negro. My name's Charley Grant."

"I *know* you're a Negro!" McGraw shouted. "But Negroes ain't allowed to play, so from now on you're a Cherokee. And your name is Chief Tokahoma. You got that?"

"Yes, sir."

I looked over at Jim. His eyes were almost bugging out of his head, like he couldn't believe what he was hearing.

"Wait a minute," he said. "You're gonna pretend this guy is an Indian so he can play, but meanwhile I'm a *real* Indian and you won't let *me* play?"

"That's right, Thorpe," McGraw said. "And you know why?"

"Why?" Jim asked.

"Because Chief Tokahoma here can hit a curve-ball."

"That's it," Jim shouted. "I quit!"

"Good!" McGraw said. "If you quit, I don't have to pay you to sit on the bench for three years."

"I hope you finish in last place!" Jim yelled, as he grabbed a shirt out of his locker. He was still buttoning it when he stormed out the door and slammed it behind him.

It was quiet for a few seconds. John McGraw shook his head and massaged his temples with two fingers.

"He'll be back," he said. "They all come back. And we'll finish in first place . . . if my brains hold out."

13

No Fighting

AFTER JIM STORMED OUT OF THE LOCKER ROOM, JOHN McGraw strolled back to his office as if nothing had happened. The players went back to preparing for the day's game.

I looked at Bobby and he looked at me. We both felt sorry for Jim, but there was nothing we could do for him now. There was no reason to stay in 1913 either.

But then again, there was no reason we had to get home right away.

"Let's blow this pop stand," Bobby said, jerking his head toward the door.

There were lots of twists and turns in the tunnels under the Polo Grounds. It was amazing that we ever found our way out of the place. Eventually we discovered a door that led to the street. By that time, Jim Thorpe was long gone.

"How are we gonna find him?" I asked Bobby. The street was full of people rushing in all directions.

"I have a hunch I know where Jim's heading," he said, and we took off down Eighth Avenue.

I had been to New York before. I visited Babe Ruth there in 1932 and Jackie Robinson in 1947. But this was decades earlier. It looked like a completely different city.

There *was* a skyline in the distance, but it was kind of wimpy, if you ask me. The Empire State Building didn't exist yet. Most of the "skyscrapers" were less than ten stories high.

Without tall buildings, you could actually *see* the sky, and there were no planes flying around. The Wright brothers had only gotten off the ground a few years earlier. There *were* cars in the street, but there were also a lot of horse-drawn buggies. You had to be careful with every step you took, because where there are horses, there's horse manure.

"This is my kinda place!" Bobby said.

Bobby acted like he knew where he was going, so I followed him. The street was a buzz of activity. Men with straw hats and mustaches were everywhere. It was like that was their uniform. Women wore huge floppy hats with flowers on top. Restaurants advertised dinner for 15 cents. There were pushcarts selling all kinds of stuff. I saw a guy lifting a big block of ice out of a truck and rolling it up somebody's front steps. I guess people didn't even have refrigerators yet.

There were lots of movie theaters, showing films like *The Last Days of Pompeii* and *Dr. Jekyll and Mr. Hyde*. I wondered if they were silent movies. There were live theaters too, and each one featured an assortment of sword swallowers, fire breathers, glass eaters, and other weird acts: The Amazing Tomsoni and His Trick Bicyclists. The Duncan Twins. Buck and Bubbles.

"This is my kinda place!" Bobby said.

We had walked a couple of blocks when Bobby pulled me into a doorway with a sign over it that said EIGHTH AVENUE SALOON.

"Wait!" I said, stopping at the door. "This is a bar!"

"Duh!"

"Kids aren't allowed in bars," I protested.

"Will you relax, Stoshack?" Bobby said. "It's okay as long as we don't drink. My parents took me to Las Vegas once, and kids were allowed in the casino as long as they didn't gamble. Same thing. Just look like you belong."

He was right. Nobody paid any attention to us at all.

There was sawdust on the floor, and a big sign that said NO FIGHTING! I noticed an autographed picture of Jim Thorpe on the wall, and photos of the other Giants too.

"Look!" Bobby said. "There he is."

Jim was at the bar with a drink in his hand and two empty glasses in front of him. Three guys wearing bowler hats surrounded him. We muscled our way over until we were close enough to hear them.

"So what did you say when the king of Sweden put that gold medal around your neck?" one of the guys asked Jim.

"Thanks, King!" Jim said, and the three guys roared with laughter. Jim leaned his head back and downed the drink. One of the guys signaled to the bartender to bring Jim another one. He did, and then said he had to get a new bottle from the cellar. It looked like Jim was a regular in this place.

"He's drinking like a fish!" I told Bobby.

Jim had started telling a story about the Olympics, when some other guy staggered over to the group. He was a big guy, and he wasn't dressed nicely like the other three. He had on an undershirt that showed off his muscles.

"Ain't you Jim Thorpe?" the guy asked.

"So they say," Jim said, taking a swig of his drink.

"I hear you're one tough Indian," the guy said.

"They say that too."

"Well, you don't look so tough to *me*."

"Maybe not," Jim said, turning to get a good look at the guy.

"You know how to box?" the guy asked.

"A little," Jim replied, turning back to the bar.

"I bet I could knock you down."

A hush fell over the bar as Jim turned to look the guy over again. Then he reached into his pocket and pulled out a hundred-dollar bill. Somebody gasped. A hundred must have been like a *fortune* in 1913.

"Tell you what," Jim said, slapping the bill on the bar. "I'll give you one punch. If you knock me down, you keep this hundred."

Jim was slurring his words. There was no way he should be making bets when he was drunk. I felt like I should do something, but I didn't know what.

"I'll take that bet," the guy said, pumping a fist into his hand.

"But if you *don't* knock me down," Jim continued, "I get *your* hundred and a punch of my own."

"I ain't got no hundred," the guy said.

Everybody at the bar rushed to pull bills out of their wallets. One of the guys counted up the money. When he reached a hundred dollars, he put the bills on top of Jim's hundred-dollar bill.

"Okay," Jim said, as he got off the barstool and clasped his hands behind his back. "Your turn."

Then the guy with the muscles smiled and made

a big show out of rolling his shoulders. Everybody stopped what they were doing.

The guy reared back and walloped Jim right in the stomach, really hard. His fist made a sound like a fastball slamming into a catcher's mitt.

A punch like that would have knocked me back at least ten feet. It would have put me in the hospital, for sure.

Jim grimaced a little and just stood there. Then he smiled. All the guys in the bar started whispering to each other.

"Okay," Jim said. "My turn."

Without any warmup, Jim socked the guy in the jaw.

The guy's head turned with the punch. He fell backward and hit the floor like a sack of potatoes. His eyes were shut. He wasn't going to be bothering anybody for a long time.

I'll tell you, if the cell phone had been invented, every one of those guys in the bar would have been calling his friends to tell them what happened. They were all yelling and offering toasts and clapping Jim on the back. He calmly picked up the bills off the bar and stuffed them in his pocket.

That was when the bartender came back up from the cellar. He had a bottle in one hand, and a gun in the other.

"What's goin' on?" he asked, looking at the guy on the floor. "There's no fighting in this saloon."

"Jimmy just taught that fella a lesson," one of the

guys in a bowler hat said.

"You've had enough," the bartender said to Jim. "I'm gonna have to ask you to leave . . . again."

"Just one more drink," Jim said, "and I'll be on my way."

"Do you know who you're talking to?" another guy asked the bartender. "That's Jim Thorpe, the Olympic champion!"

"I know who he is," replied the bartender, pointing the gun at Jim. "I don't care if he's Woodrow Wilson. No fighting in this bar."

"There was no fight!" yelled Bobby. "Jim just punched that guy's lights out."

Everybody turned to look at Bobby. Even Jim.

"Who are *you*?" asked the bartender.

"I'm Jim Thorpe's great-grandson," Bobby said, which were probably the stupidest words anyone in the world has ever uttered. Some of the guys at the bar laughed. Jim wasn't even thirty years old.

"Well, you better get Grandpa outta here by the time I count to five, or he's gonna have a hole in his head big enough to put a baseball through," the bartender said. "One . . . two . . ."

Jim wasn't making any move to leave.

"You think I'm kidding? Three . . . four . . . five."

14

On the Sidewalks
of New York

ME AND BOBBY GRABBED JIM BY HIS SHOULDERS AND hustled him to the door. We had to hold him up. He was so drunk I was afraid he was going to fall over.

"Come on," Bobby told Jim once we were out on the street. "We'll help you get home."

"I didn't know I had a great-grandson," Jim muttered. "I'm not even married yet."

"We live in the twenty-first century," Bobby explained. "My friend Stosh here can travel through time . . . with baseball cards."

Jim looked at us funny, like he was trying to focus his eyes.

"Here, I can prove it," Bobby said, pulling the iPod out of his backpack. "Stick these things in your ears."

"What are they?" Jim asked.

"Earbuds."

Jim stuck them in his ears and Bobby turned on the iPod. Jim instantly let out a scream and fell to the sidewalk, ripping the earbuds out.

"Turn it *down*!" I told Bobby.

"It was in my head!" Jim yelled. "The sound was in my head! What *was* that?"

"Heavy metal," Bobby told him

After Jim had recovered, he got up and examined the iPod carefully. It was like he couldn't believe that such a little thing could make such a big noise.

"Can I hear that again?" he asked.

Bobby gave him the earbuds and turned the iPod on again, lowering the volume this time.

"Pretty cool, huh?" Bobby asked.

Jim didn't hear him. He was bobbing his head up and down with the music.

"This is good," Jim said when the song ended. "Twenty-first century, huh?"

Jim must have liked the iPod, because he put an arm around each of us, and we all started walking down Eighth Avenue together. I think the blast of music sobered him up a little.

"Hey, what's the deal with John McGraw?" I asked, stepping over some horse manure in the street. "He is one bad guy."

"There's an old Indian saying," Jim said. "Bad in good, and good in bad."

"How come he hates you so much?" asked Bobby.

"I like to win," Jim said, "but with McGraw, nothing else matters. *Nothing*. Winning is his whole life. I like to compete; if I don't win all the time, that's okay. McGraw can't tolerate failure. Ever. I guess that's why me and him don't get along."

"So why don't you become a free agent?" Bobby suggested.

"A *what*?" asked Jim.

"A free agent," Bobby said. "You sign with whichever team offers you the most money."

Jim leaned back and roared, as if he'd heard a great joke.

I'm sure Bobby had no idea that free agency didn't exist until the 1970s. Before that, the team that signed a player *owned* him until they released him or traded him. Jim was stuck with the Giants until they decided to get rid of him. That's why baseball players used to play their whole career with one team. Now, hardly anybody does.

I looked in the windows as we walked down Eighth Avenue. There were no stores selling electronics, like we have today. Electronics didn't exist yet. There were no video stores. No computer stores. No supermarkets. No fast-food chains. But there were plenty of hat stores and butchers and newsstands. A little gift shop had part of its display devoted to Christy Mathewson. It had Matty sweaters. Matty playing cards. Matty board games. There were plenty of billiard parlors and bars. I was afraid that Jim was looking for a place to get another drink.

"Hey, Thorpe!" a guy on the street suddenly shouted as he passed. "You're a bum!"

"*All* ballplayers are bums," said the lady with him. "The Olympics are over. Get a job, you shirker."

Jim ignored them. We had walked maybe ten blocks from the bar, and I could tell that many of the people on the street recognized Jim. Some would just nod their heads, or look at him a little longer than they would look at a stranger.

"Excuse me?" a woman with a little girl said, stopping right in front of us. "Are you Jim Thorpe?"

"Sure am, ma'am," Jim said, taking a bow.

"We're hungry," said the little girl.

"Hush, Olivia!" said her mother.

The girl, I noticed, had dirt on her knees, and her clothes were old and frayed. Her mother was young, but her hair was messy and she looked like she hadn't slept in a long time.

Jim bent down to talk to the little girl.

"Nobody should be hungry," he said, "least of all a pretty girl like you."

Jim reached into his pocket and pulled out the money he had made beating up that guy in the bar. Then he pressed a bunch of bills into the mother's hand. Her eyes opened wide, like she had never seen so much money in her life.

"I'll pay you back," she said. "I promise. What's your address?"

"Forget it," Jim told her.

"I'll send the money to the Polo Grounds," the lady said.

Jim didn't seem to care one way or another. I couldn't believe he would just hand 200 dollars to a complete stranger.

"Why'd you do that?" I asked as we walked away.

"She needs it more than I do," he said.

At the next corner, a couple of guys were sitting forlornly on the curb next to their car, which had a flat tire. There was a spare next to them, but they weren't putting it on the car. Jim went over to them.

"Whatsa matter, boys?" he asked.

"We ain't got no jack," one of them said, "on account of Jack here lost it."

"Jack lost the jack?" asked Jim. "You can't very well jack up a car if Jack lost the jack, can you, Jack?"

"Nope," said Jack.

"How long you think it would take you boys to change that tire if you had a jack?" Jim asked.

"A minute or two," Jack said.

"Well, I'm no jack," Jim said, rolling up his sleeves, "but I reckon I can jack up your car for a minute or two."

"Are you crazy, mister?" Jack said.

"Maybe," replied Jim as he walked around to the front of the car. "You fellows get ready to work fast."

Jim leaned over and grabbed the front bumper of the car with both hands. Then he spread his legs apart and lifted up the car like a weightlifter picking up a set of barbells. The front wheels were about five inches off the ground. Instantly, a crowd gathered around to watch.

The two guys frantically took off the flat tire while Jim held the car up. Me and Bobby rushed to help. The four of us looked like the pit crew at a NASCAR race.

"Hurry it up, boys!" Jim said, sweat beading on his forehead. "I can't hold this thing up all day."

Finally, we got the spare tire on, and Jim lowered the front of the car. The crowd on the street erupted in cheers. The two guys thanked Jim about a dozen times and tried to give him money, but he wouldn't take it.

"You fellas need it more than I do," he said.

Jim told us he was staying at a hotel a few blocks away until he could get his own place. He said we didn't need to walk him the rest of the way. But Bobby wanted to, and Jim said he didn't mind the company.

There was a little newsstand on the corner, and Jim went in to buy a paper. Bobby and I looked at the candy. It was cool because they had candy bars we'd never heard of, like Goo Goo Clusters. But there were no Milky Ways. No 3 Musketeers. No Kit Kats. How did these people survive without Kit Kats?

Next to the candy rack was a shelf filled with New York Giants souvenirs. Just about every item was endorsed by Christy Mathewson. There were

Matty razors, Matty pen-and-pencil sets, Matty pipe tobacco, and so on.

Matty's name was on just about everything in the store.

"Look, he even wrote a book," Bobby said, holding up a book titled *Pitching in a Pinch*.

Jim paid for his newspaper and came over.

"Matty didn't write no book," he said. "Some *other* guy wrote it and Matty put his name on it. That's the way it works. They can stick Matty's name on any old thing and sell it. He doesn't have to do a thing except count up the loot."

"Do they ever put *your* name on stuff?" Bobby asked.

"They were going to, right after the Olympics," Jim said. "Then my medals were taken away."

"That sucks," Bobby said. "They slap Matty's name on every piece of crap there is."

"Matty's the all-American boy," I said.

"Let me tell you something," Jim said, leaning close enough so I could smell the alcohol on his breath. "My people settled in this country long before any white men arrived. My ancestors have been here for thousands of years. I'm more American than anybody. And you know what? They won't even give me American citizenship. Talk about not fair."

As soon as we left the newsstand, I noticed a crowd of people gathered down the block. Jim hustled over. I thought maybe there had been an accident or he was going to help somebody who was hurt.

But it was nothing like that. The crowd was gathered outside the offices of a newspaper, *The New York Evening Journal*. There was a huge board mounted on the side of the building. It looked sort of like a baseball scoreboard. Instead of just showing the score though, it also showed what was going on at the game.

"Strike *two*!" a guy shouted into a megaphone. "That's one ball and two strikes on Max Carey."

There was a baseball-diamond shape on the board, with cutouts of little runners at first and second base.

Lightbulbs indicated the inning, as well as the number of balls, strikes, outs, hits, runs, and errors.

"Strike him out, Matty!" some guy yelled, as if Matty could hear him. "He's a bum."

It was the Giants game at the Polo Grounds. They were playing the Pittsburgh Pirates. The Giants had a 2-1 lead in the third inning. About a hundred people were standing around "watching the game." Or a simulation of it anyway.

"Foul ball!" shouted the guy with the megaphone.

"Oh man, this is lame," Bobby whispered to me. "These people need high-def TV *bad*."

Personally, I thought it was cool.

"How does the guy with the megaphone know what's going on at the Polo Grounds?" I asked Jim.

"I thought you boys were from the future," Jim said. "Don't you know how a telegraph works?"

Of *course*! There must have been a telegraph operator at the Polo Grounds who was watching the game and tapping out the action, pitch by pitch, on a telegraph key. He sent it by wire over to the newspaper office, where it got posted almost instantly on the board. It was almost like watching the game on TV. They didn't have television, but they had this. It was pretty ingenious, in a low-tech way.

"Ball two!" shouted the megaphone man.

People in the crowd were buzzing as if they were watching the real game. One guy said Matty was sure to work his way out of the jam. Another said he wasn't the dominating pitcher he had been in his younger days.

It was taking a long time for the megaphone man to make an announcement. The crowd seemed to be getting restless. It occurred to me that no news was most likely bad news. It probably meant that something exciting had happened, and the telegraph operator at the Polo Grounds needed more time to describe it.

"It's a base hit!" shouted the megaphone man suddenly. The little batter on the board moved toward first base. The little runners started to move toward the next bases.

"No!" screamed the crowd.

"It's a double!" shouted the megaphone man.

"NO!" screamed the crowd.

"Two runs score!" shouted the megaphone man. Both of the little runners crossed home plate. The score was 3-2, in favor of Pittsburgh.

"Noooooooooo!" screamed the crowd.

Jim turned suddenly and headed back down the street in the direction we had come from.

"Where are you going?" Bobby yelled after him.

"The boys are losing," he said. "They might need me. Come on!"

15

Inside Baseball

"THE POLO GROUNDS!" JIM ORDERED THE CAB DRIVER. "And step on it!"

It was one of those old Model T cars, with tires that weren't much fatter than the ones on my bike. Jim climbed in the front seat. Bobby and I jumped in the back.

"This Tin Lizzie will do 40 miles per hour, sir!" bragged the driver.

Bobby and I looked at each other and tried not to laugh. 40 miles an hour?! That was it? But when the driver hit the gas, we wiped those grins off our faces. He was weaving around the other cars and horses like a maniac. Every time the cab swerved, we bounced around the backseat like a couple of Ping-Pong balls.

"Where are the seat belts?" Bobby yelled.

"The *what*?" Jim replied.

I told Bobby they didn't have seat belts in 1913, and we grabbed onto whatever we could to avoid being thrown out of the cab. Somehow, we made it back to the Polo Grounds without getting killed.

When Jim opened the cab door, I could hear a brass band playing that old song that goes "East side, west side, all around the town." People inside the ballpark were banging pots, pans, and cowbells. The smell of roasted peanuts was in the air.

"These boys are with me," Jim told the guard as we rushed through the turnstile.

Jim dashed through the winding tunnels under the ballpark. He ran with a natural grace, like a deer. Bobby and I were huffing and puffing to keep up.

"When you run," Jim said, "you draw strength from the four directions—north, south, east, and west. That strength helps you meet the challenges you face."

"What does that mean?" Bobby asked me.

"Beats me," I said.

We were just about to collapse when Jim stopped and opened a door. It led directly into the Giants' dugout. John McGraw was standing there.

"I knew you'd be back," McGraw barked. "Who the hell are these guttersnipes?"

"Mr. McGraw," Jim said, "there's an old Indian superstition that children bring luck."

"Well, get 'em in here," McGraw ordered. "We need all the luck we can get. What's that I smell on your breath, Thorpe? Whiskey? That'll cost you another hundred bucks. Now get your uniform on!"

Jim ran to the locker room. Bobby and I grabbed some bench. Even though I had been in major league dugouts before, it was still a thrill. I was watching Christy Mathewson, John McGraw, and the 1913 New York Giants! It was like a dream come true.

Bobby had this look on his face like a kid in a candy store. It was so different from the scowl he always carried around back home.

"How cool is this?" I whispered.

"Way cool," Bobby said.

I looked at the scoreboard. It was the bottom of the sixth inning. Pittsburgh was still leading, 3-2. The Pirates were jogging out to the field and the Giants were coming into the dugout. Christy Mathewson sat down next to me, slapping his glove on the bench. He didn't look too happy. Nobody likes losing.

The Pirates whipped the ball around the infield. It was pretty much like watching a modern team warm up, except for two things. First, the ball wasn't white anymore. It was sort of dirty brown. Second, the gloves were tiny! I couldn't imagine how anybody could catch a ball whizzing at you with a glove that wasn't much bigger than your hand. But they were doing it, and well. They never dropped the ball.

The shortstop looked familiar to me. He was a husky guy with bowed legs.

"Excuse me," I said to Matty, "who's that guy at short?"

I could swear I had seen that guy somewhere before.

Matty looked at me like I must be a total idiot.

"You never heard of Honus Wagner?" he said.

Honus Wagner? Of course! Not only had I heard of him, but I had even *met* him before. The first time I traveled through time, it was with a 1909 Honus Wagner card. But that's a story for another day.

A guy with a huge megaphone walked back and forth in foul territory behind home plate.

"Now batting for the Giants," he bellowed, "Red Murray."

After looking at a couple of pitches, Murray grounded out to short. So did the next batter. Honus scooped each ball up in his huge hands and fired it like a bullet, peppering the first baseman with dirt and pebbles along with the ball.

"Man, Wagner's got a gun for an arm," Bobby said.

Jim Thorpe, now in uniform, stepped into the dugout through the back door. He sat between me and Bobby.

"Two outs," I told him.

"Now batting for the Giants," the megaphone man shouted, "Fred Merkle."

Merkle didn't care *what* the pitcher did to the ball.

While Merkle was walking up to the plate, the pitcher stepped off the mound, leaned over, and spit on the baseball.

"Did you see that?" Bobby said.

"See what?" asked Jim.

"That guy just spit on the ball!"

"Yeah, so?"

"Isn't that illegal?" asked Bobby.

The players on the bench all turned and looked at Bobby like he was crazy.

Bobby doesn't know much about baseball history. I whispered to him that the spitball wasn't banned until 1920. He slapped his forehead.

But Fred Merkle didn't care *what* the pitcher did to the ball. He whacked a drive into the gap that went all the way to the rightfield wall. By the time the Pirates got the ball in, Merkle was chugging to third base. The Giants fans went crazy. "Go back to Peoria, busher!" a fan yelled at the pitcher. "Adams, you stink!"

John McGraw hopped off the bench and went to coach third.

McGraw went out to coach third base.

He was a riot to watch. He was yelling encouragement, jumping around, taking off his cap, putting it back on, patting his head, and touching his ears. If you didn't know he was coaching third and flashing signs to his players, you'd swear he was one of those crazy people you see on the street.

"Now batting for the Giants, Larry Doyle!"

Doyle didn't swing at the first pitch, but the umpire jumped up dramatically to call it a strike.

"You have to learn, before you're older," the ump hollered in a singsong voice. "You can't hit with the bat on your shoulder."

The next pitch looked good. Doyle took a healthy cut at it, but missed.

"It cut the middle of the plate," sang the umpire. "But you missed 'cause you swung late."

"What's up with that ump?" I asked Jim.

"That dude is annoying," Bobby added.

"That's Lord Byron," replied Jim. "They call him the Singing Umpire."

With a runner at third, and two outs and two strikes on the batter, the Giants were desperate to score the tying run. That's when John McGraw did something I'd never seen before.

"Hey, Adams!" he yelled to the pitcher from the third base line. "Lemme see that ball for a second, will ya?"

The pitcher looked over at McGraw, who was holding out his hands to catch the ball. Adams hesitated for maybe half a second, then he shrugged and flipped the ball underhanded to McGraw. But instead of catching it, McGraw simply stepped aside and let the ball roll down the third base line.

"Go!" McGraw shouted to Merkle at third, and everybody in the dugout started yelling, "GO! GO! GO!" Merkle didn't need the advice. He took off and crossed the plate standing up.

"Awesome!" shouted Bobby, who got up and tried to give Merkle a high five as he jogged into the dugout. Merkle looked at Bobby like he was from Neptune.

The Pirates' manager ran over to Lord Byron and started shouting at him.

"That's illegal!" he argued. "You ain't allowed to do that. It's a dead ball!"

"Look in the book and read the rule," Lord Byron sang. "If you throw away the ball, you're a fool."

John McGraw didn't join the argument. He came back to the dugout chuckling to himself.

"Oldest trick in the book," he said to the guys on the bench.

That run tied the game. The next Giant struck out to end the inning.

Matty grabbed his glove and went out to pitch the seventh. I watched him warm up. He had a nice, easy, graceful delivery. It looked like he wasn't even trying. But the ball moved so fast, it was nearly invisible after leaving his hand. It popped in the catcher's mitt with a BANG you could hear across the ballpark.

**When Matty was throwing the ball,
it didn't even look like he was trying.**

Most of the Giants were out in the field now, with the exception of Jim Thorpe and Charley Grant, that black guy who McGraw was trying to pass off as an Indian.

"How about putting me in there, Mr. McGraw?" asked Jim.

"You'll get in when I say so," McGraw snapped.

While Matty was warming up, McGraw had his head in a book titled *Rules of Baseball.*

"Gee, I would think you'd know that stuff by now, Mr. McGraw," Charley Grant said.

"I know it by heart," said McGraw, jotting down a note on one of the pages.

"So why are you reading the rules?"

"To figure out how to break 'em," McGraw replied.

The Pirates' leadoff batter slapped down at the ball and hit a high hopper wide of the first base bag. Fred Merkle grabbed it and arrived at first the same time as the batter. They collided, falling on top of each other. The ump called the batter safe. Runner on first, nobody out.

"Fadeaway, Matty!" some of the fans chanted when play resumed. "Fadeaway!"

"What's a fadeaway?" Bobby whispered to me.

"That's what they used to call a screwball," I told him.

I knew the fadeaway was Matty's signature pitch. Instead of twisting his wrist *out* as he released the ball, he twisted it *in*. It made a reverse curve that broke toward a right-handed batter. It's very hard to throw, because our wrists don't twist in naturally.

The next Pirate squared around to bunt, and dropped one down on the right side of the infield. Matty rushed in and whipped the ball to second for the force out. The runner flung his body at the base, taking out the shortstop before he could even think about throwing to first for a double play. One out. Still a runner at first.

This, I knew, is the way baseball *used* to be played back in the Dead Ball days. It was very hard to hit a ball out of the park, so teams would choke up, bunt, slap at the ball, steal bases, hit and run, or rely on their wits to score runs. And if all else failed, they'd cheat. It was called "inside baseball."

Personally, I liked it better than the modern game. I always thought watching a home run go over the wall was boring. I'd rather see a guy hit a triple and watch runners tearing around the bases while the defense scramble to relay the ball in and throw them out. *That's* exciting.

"Did the Giants win their division last year?" Bobby asked me.

"There are no divisions," I told him. "There's just an American League and a National League."

"So they don't have playoffs?"

"No playoffs."

"No wild card?"

"No," I told him. "You finish in first place, or you go home."

"Wow," Bobby said. "No wonder they play so hard."

The next batter fouled Matty's first pitch into the third base stands. I assumed the umpire would throw Matty a new ball, but he didn't. Instead, some big guy ran into the stands and grabbed the ball away from the fan who caught it. What a jerk!

But the guy who stole the ball didn't keep it or run away with it. He threw it back to Matty. That's when I remembered that in 1913, fans weren't allowed to keep foul balls that went into the stands. The guy was only doing his job.

They had been using the same baseball for the whole game. No wonder it wasn't white anymore. It was brown and scuffed up, covered with spit, dirt, and who knows what else. And these guys were expected to hit it and throw it accurately.

The Pirates scored a run in the eighth inning to go ahead 4-3, and that was still the score when the Giants came up to bat in the bottom of the ninth.

Buck Herzog led off for the Giants, slapping a single past the second baseman. The next guy, Red Murray, bunted, but the Pirates' catcher pounced on the ball and whipped it to second. There was a collision there, and Lord Byron called Herzog out.

Well, John McGraw went nuts. He ran out of the dugout and stuck his face right into Lord Byron's.

"Get some glasses, you fobbing, swag-bellied hedge pig!" he shouted. "My man was safe, you loggerheaded, toad-spotted maggot pie!"

"You got 60 seconds to state your case," sang Lord Byron, as he pulled one of those old-time watches out of his pocket. "Then it's time to shut your face."

McGraw didn't use his 60 seconds. He snatched Lord Byron's watch, threw it on the ground, and stomped on it.

The fans went crazy. Some people started throwing vegetables onto the field. I guess they brought them to the ballpark just so they could throw them. Strange.

"McGraw, I'd say you're out of luck," sang Lord Byron. "That'll cost a hundred bucks!"

"It was worth it!" McGraw said as he stomped back to the dugout.

Matty was due up next, but with the Giants

down by a run in the bottom of the ninth, McGraw was looking toward the bench for a pinch hitter. Jim grabbed a bat and slid forward, trying to catch the manager's eye.

"Chief Tokahoma!" barked McGraw. "Grab a bat!"

Jim slammed his bat back into the rack while Charley Grant jumped off the bench.

"Pinch hitting for the Giants," announced the megaphone man, "from the Cherokee nation, Chief . . . Tokahoma!"

Charley headed for home plate. But before he got ten feet out of the dugout, the Pirates' manager was out on the field, shouting at the umpire.

"That man is no Cherokee!" he yelled. "He's a Negro!"

A gasp came out of the crowd.

Lord Byron went over to Charley and put a hand on his shoulder.

"Son," the ump said, "what's your name?"

"Charley Grant, sir."

"Now tell me the truth," Lord Byron said. "Are you an Indian?"

"No, sir," Charley admitted.

"I'm sorry," said Lord Byron, "but you're not allowed here. Nothin' personal, mind you."

Charley lowered his head and walked back to the Giants' dugout.

"I told you to say you were Chief Tokahoma!" shouted John McGraw. "You do as I tell you!"

Charley didn't sit down when he got to the

bench. He just dropped his bat, opened the door behind the dugout, and left. He didn't say a word, and nobody said a word to him.

It was awfully quiet in the Polo Grounds. Bobby and I knew something that nobody else in the ballpark knew. It would be more than 30 years until professional baseball would let a black man—Jackie Robinson—on the field.

16

The Indian in the
Batter's Box

"MR. MCGRAW, PUT UP A BATTER!" ORDERED LORD BYRON. "I'm tired of watching you get fatter!"

McGraw looked up and down the bench. He didn't have much of a choice. It's not like he was going to send me or Bobby to the plate.

"Thorpe!" he hollered. "Grab a bat." Then he turned to Lord Byron and said, "If *this* guy ain't Indian, nobody is."

Jim picked one of the smaller bats out of the rack. Some of the fans started chanting Indian war whoops as he walked to the plate. Jim wasn't smiling. He looked determined. Finally, he was getting a chance to hit.

"Pinch-hitting for the Giants," announced the megaphone man, "winner of the Olympic decath-

Jim had an odd batting stance.

lon . . . the greatest all-around athlete in the world
. . . JIM THORPE!"

The fans made more Indian whoops as Jim
stepped into the batter's box. He stood toward the
front of the box, with his feet close together and his
bat held down low. It was an odd stance. He pumped
the bat across the plate a few times.

The first pitch to Jim was a big, old, lazy curve.
He took a wild swing at it, spinning around in the
batter's box. Strike one.

The pitcher smirked and threw the exact same pitch. Again, Jim missed it. I swear, it looked like I could hit those curveballs. Strike two.

The fans were yelling at Jim now. I wondered if he was still feeling the effect of all that whiskey he drank earlier. Or maybe he just couldn't hit a curveball, drunk or sober.

The pitcher tried to waste the next pitch off the outside corner. But Jim reached over and slapped at it, tapping a little dribbler down the third base line. It was like a swinging bunt.

Thorpe took off like a rocket for first base. I never saw a man accelerate so fast in all my life.

It looked like the ball was going to roll foul, but just before it touched the base line it swerved back into fair territory. The third baseman rushed in to barehand the ball, but he had no play. Jim was already at first.

Red Murray, who had been the runner on first, saw the third baseman charge in to field the ball. He knew that nobody was covering third. So he didn't stop at second. He made it all the way to third on Jim's infield hit.

I glanced over at Bobby, and he put up his hand for a high five. I slapped it. If we hadn't sloped the base line before the game, Jim's infield hit would have been a foul ball.

"Now batting for the Giants," announced the megaphone man, "Fred Snodgrass."

The crowd was buzzing. *This* was what baseball

was all about, in any century. Bottom of the ninth, with the home team down by a run. Runners at first and third. Only one out. A single would tie the game. With Jim's speed at first base, a double could win it. The momentum had shifted to the Giants. There was the feeling of anticipation in the Polo Grounds. The fans could taste a victory.

Near third base, John McGraw was furiously hopping around, blowing his nose, flashing signs, and touching about a dozen different parts of his body. It looked like he was doing the Macarena out there.

Snodgrass dug in at the plate. If the Giants won, he'd be the hero of the day. Murray edged off third base. Jim took a lead off first. The pitcher stared in for the sign from his catcher. He started his windup.

Then, suddenly, Jim broke for second!

"He's going!" shouted the catcher.

Instead of throwing a pitch, the pitcher wheeled around and fired the ball to second. At shortstop, Honus Wagner ran over to take the throw. He slapped the tag on Jim's foot.

"Yer out!" hollered Lord Byron.

Murray, seeing the pitcher spin toward second, figured he had a shot to steal home, and he took off from third. But Honus was no ordinary shortstop. As soon as he tagged Jim out, he jumped up and fired the ball to the plate. Murray was out by three feet.

"Yer out!" hollered Lord Byron. "I call that a double play! And you boys can call it a day."

The Pirates had won, and the Giants fans didn't

like it one bit. More vegetables came flying out of the stands. Snodgrass flung his bat away in disgust. He never got the chance to drive in the winning run. And John McGraw, well, he just about *exploded*.

"What are you, Thorpe, stupid?" he yelled. "Who told you to steal second?"

"*You* did!" Thorpe yelled right back at him. "You blew your nose. That's the steal sign."

"That was the steal sign *last* week, you milk-livered maggot pie!"

"But I thought—" Jim started.

"You thought?" yelled McGraw. "Who told you to think? You're supposed to follow instructions! Thinking is *my* job and I'll take the heat if we lose! Maybe you'd remember the signs if you didn't spend all your time getting drunk!"

A couple of tomatoes hit Jim on the back as he walked slowly, head down, toward the dugout.

"Go back to the Olympics, Thorpe!" some guy yelled.

"Go back to the reservation," yelled another fan.

"Ah, leave the guy alone," shouted a lady. "He's a savage. He probably can't even read."

Without a word, Jim clomped into the dugout and opened the door to the locker room.

"Where are you going?" McGraw yelled after him. "I'm not finished with you!"

"I'm going home," Jim replied glumly. "I quit."

"Again?" MrGraw shouted. "Well, go ahead! That's what you are, Thorpe—a quitter! Get out of my sight! You disgust me!"

This time, Jim Thorpe didn't lash out and attack John McGraw. Nobody needed to hold him back from punching the manager. There was no fight left in him.

17

Meeting with an Old Friend

MAYBE JIM THORPE *WAS* THE GREATEST ALL-AROUND athlete in the world. But that didn't mean he was a good baseball player.

That's one of the interesting things about the game. You can run fast, jump high, have muscles out to here, and *still* be lousy. I knew that Michael Jordan was one of the greatest athletes in the world. After nine seasons of professional basketball, he decided to try and make it as a baseball player. He barely hit .200—and that was in the *minor* leagues. Baseball isn't like other sports. It requires a special set of skills, and very few people have them.

There was nothing Bobby and I could do for Jim. But before going back home, there was one thing I wanted to do for myself. I told Bobby to give me a few minutes. Then I jogged across the infield to the

Pirates' dugout. It didn't take me long to find Honus Wagner, packing his bats and glove into an equipment bag.

"Excuse me, Mr. Wagner," I said.

Honus turned around. I didn't expect him to recognize me. Kids probably pestered him all the time.

"Do you need an autograph, son?" he asked gently, reaching for a pen.

"No, sir," I said, "I just wanted to say hello. We met once before, in 1909. Back in Louisville. Remember? I was the kid who—"

"Stosh!" Honus exclaimed. "Sure, I remember you! The kid who travels through time. You back again?"

"I came to see Jim Thorpe," I told him.

"He's a good man," Honus said, shaking his head sadly. "It must have been tough on him when they took those medals away. And he can't seem to get a break out here. Playin' for McGraw ain't no picnic, I'm sure."

"They don't get along very well," I told him.

"Y'know, Stosh, ever since we met, I've been wondering something," Honus said. "How much did you get for that card with my picture on it?"

I first met Honus because I had a 1909 Honus Wagner T-206 baseball card, which is the most valuable card in the world. It was in mint condition and probably worth a million dollars. Honus couldn't believe it when I told him. It's a long story, but this jerky card-store owner named Birdie Farrell beat me up and took the card away. Then it got destroyed. I never got a dime for it.

"Somebody ripped it up," I said.

"Sorry to hear that," said Honus. "I wish I had another one for you."

"It's okay," I assured Honus. "Hey, ever since we met, *I've* been wondering something too. Whatever happened with you and that girl?"

Again, it's a long story. But when I met Honus the first time, I reunited him with his old girlfriend. In fact, *she* was the one who ripped up the baseball card. I wondered if they got married.

"What girl?" Honus asked.

"You know," I said, "Amanda Young. You called her Mandy, remember?"

"Oh, yeah!" Honus said. "Things, uh, didn't quite work out with me and Mandy."

"Sorry to hear that, Honus."

"Well, the truth is, she took a likin' to another ballplayer."

"She dumped you!?" I said, astonished. Honus was just about the nicest guy in the world. "That's impossible! What ballplayer could she possibly pick over you?"

"Well, he's a pretty good player," Honus said with a chuckle. "His name is Ty Cobb."

"Amanda Young is Ty Cobb's *girlfriend*?!"

I could hardly believe it. Ty Cobb was such a jerk. But Honus didn't seem heartbroken over it. In fact, he and I had a good laugh. It was great to see him again, but we couldn't talk long because the Pirates had to catch a train to Philadelphia for a series against the Phillies. So I shook his huge hand, wished him well, and said good-bye.

"You tell Thorpe to hang in there," Honus told me.

"I will."

"Hey Stosh!" Honus shouted as I walked away. "Tell me something. Who's gonna win the World Series this year?"

"You'll find out in October," I shouted back.

Bobby Fuller was waiting impatiently for me in the Giants' dugout. I wondered if he used the short time alone to take some of the drugs he'd been hiding in his backpack.

"What took ya so long?" he asked.

"I had to talk to an old friend," I told him. "What do you say? Are you ready to blow this pop stand?"

"No."

"What do you mean, no?" I asked. "There's nothing we can do here for Jim. The Olympics are over. They took away his medals. The scandal already happened. Let's go home."

"We can't leave now," Bobby said seriously.

"Why not?"

"I'm afraid Jim might try to kill himself," Bobby said.

Well *that* stopped me. Jim *did* look really depressed after he got caught trying to steal second and blew the game for the Giants. It was obvious that he was having a tough time getting along with John McGraw. And he did seem to have a drinking problem. But suicide? I didn't think so. In fact, I *knew* he wouldn't do that.

"Jim *can't* kill himself," I insisted. "He's not going to die until 1953. I looked it up. It's in the books."

Bobby thought about that for a moment.

"It doesn't matter if it's in the books," he said. "How do you know for sure that he wouldn't have killed himself in 1913 if we hadn't come here and stopped him?"

It was a valid point, I had to admit. There was the possibility that Jim made a suicide attempt in 1913 that was never recorded in history because it failed. If Bobby and I didn't save him, he might kill himself for real and we'd get back home to find that all the history books say Jim Thorpe committed suicide in 1913.

I had never seen Bobby Fuller look so serious before.

"Stoshack," he continued, "alcohol and suicide run in my family. My uncle killed himself a few years ago. If Jim kills himself, he won't get married and have children. And if he doesn't have children, his children won't have children. And if his children don't have children—"

"We'll get back home and you won't exist," I said. "Because you would never have been born."

"That's right," Bobby said.

We had to stop him.

18

A Bum

BOBBY AND I RUSHED THROUGH THE TURNSTILE AND OUT the front gate of the Polo Grounds, elbowing our way through the crowds. If Jim killed himself, it wouldn't be John McGraw's fault for being mean to him. It would be *our* fault for not saving him. And if we didn't save Jim, Bobby was a goner. That would be *my* fault alone, because I was the one who had brought him to 1913 in the first place.

I must admit there were times I wished Bobby Fuller would vanish off the face of the earth. But deep down inside, I didn't want to make that happen. We had our ups and downs, but he had actually been an okay time-traveling companion. I also felt sorry for him because he was addicted to drugs. And he did save my life from that wrecking ball.

We ran down Eighth Avenue to that bar where Jim had been drinking before the game. He seemed to be a regular there, so we figured he might have gone back. But when we rushed in the door, we didn't see Jim anywhere.

"Is Jim Thorpe here?" I asked the bartender breathlessly.

"I kicked him out 'bout ten minutes ago," he replied. "Drunk again."

The guy looked like he was mad. I don't get that. It's a *bar*. They sell alcohol. What do they expect to happen when people drink it? Isn't getting customers drunk the whole purpose of a bar?

"We've gotta find him!" Bobby said. "It's a matter of life and death!"

"I think Jimmy's living at the Trinity Hotel till he finds an apartment," the bartender told us. "It's ten blocks downtown. If you find him, tell him he owes me for the whiskey. I don't know what that guy does with all the money the Giants pay him. He's always broke."

I knew what he did with the money. He gave it away to total strangers on the street who needed it more than he did. We thanked the bartender and ran out of there.

It seemed like we were always late. We had been too late to stop him from entering the Olympics. And if he had any plans to kill himself, we might be too late to stop those too.

Bobby and I ran eight city blocks—I counted—when we passed a park on our right. The sun was starting to set. There was a big, grassy field, and people were strolling, walking dogs, and reading newspapers on benches. Bobby suddenly slowed down, and then stopped running entirely.

"What's the matter?" I asked. "You need a rest?"

"Look," Bobby said.

There were some boys in the park playing football. Touch football, three on three.

"You want to play football *now*?" I asked in disbelief.

"No, moron," Bobby said. "Check out the guy sitting under the tree."

It was Jim! He was alive!

Jim was watching the boys play football. We ran over and sat on the grass next to him. He was obviously drunk. I wasn't sure he could even stand up if he tried.

"Now *this* is *my* game," he said when he noticed us, slurring his words badly. "I was a two-time All-American in college, y'know."

"Jim, let us take you to your hotel," I said gently.

"I could throw a pass *90* yards," Jim continued. "When I ran with the ball, guys would try to tackle me and I'd drag 'em halfway across the field. One time I punted and ran 50 yards to catch my own punt. Those are *facts*."

"We believe you," Bobby said.

"We had this trick play we called the Dig," Jim whispered, like he didn't want anybody to hear. "Two guys would go out for a pass, one short and the other guy about ten yards deeper. The quarterback would throw a pass to the first guy, but he wouldn't catch it."

"He'd drop it on purpose?" Bobby asked.

"No," Jim said, "he'd tip it backward over his head. The defense would go to tackle him, leaving the second guy free to catch the ball and score. That's the Dig."

"It's genius!" Bobby said.

"Oldest trick in the book," said Jim.

When Jim was talking about football, a look of peace and contentment came over his face. Maybe it was the whiskey talking, but he seemed more relaxed. He almost looked like a different person.

"Why don't you quit baseball?" Bobby asked him. "That's what I did. I bet you'd be a star in the NFL."

"The *what*?" Jim asked.

Of course Jim couldn't join the NFL, I realized. There *was* no NFL in 1913. There was no NBA or NHL either. There were basically two sports athletes could earn money playing—baseball and boxing.

The brief peaceful look on Jim's face vanished when he turned away from watching the football game. His eyes got all squinty and bitter again.

"Six months ago everybody called me the greatest athlete in the world," he said. "Now they call me a bum."

"You're not a bum," I told him.

"Whenever I mess up, they say my brain isn't as smart as a white man's," Jim said. "And when I do good, they say I'm a savage who was raised with a fighting spirit. But I'm just a man, like any other."

Jim may have been drunk, but I didn't doubt the truth of what he was saying.

"The white man stereotyped Indians to justify killing us and stealing our land," Bobby said.

"Baseball and money ruined my life," Jim went on. "Playing ball for money before the Olympics ruined me. Now it's ruining me again."

We needed to get him home. Maybe a good sleep would snap him out of it. But Jim just wanted to talk, so we let him.

"Y'know, one day in semi-pro I hit three homers in one game, and I hit 'em in three different states."

"That's impossible," Bobby said, rolling his eyes.

"We were playing a few miles from Texarkana, close to the border," Jim said. "In the first inning, I hit a ball over the leftfield wall and it landed in Oklahoma. In the third inning, I hit one over the rightfield wall that landed in Arkansas. Then, in the seventh inning, I hit an inside-the-park homer. That was in Texas. Three states. Nobody ever did that before or since, and that's a *fact*. Of course, those pitchers couldn't break off a big yellow yakker like the boys do up here."

"Yakker?" I asked.

"Curveball," he replied.

"Is that your whole problem?" I asked. "Hitting the curve?"

"I hit the straight ones just fine," Jim said. "But

once they found out I couldn't hit the curve, I never saw any more straight ones. And McGraw won't give me the chance to learn."

"I know how to hit a curve!" I said, getting up off the grass. "I can show you."

"You're just a kid," Jim said.

"Oh, Stoshack is good," Bobby said, and that was probably the nicest thing he ever said about me. "He can teach you."

Jim struggled to get up and then crossed his arms over his chest, like he didn't believe I could teach him anything. But I told him everything I knew about the curve—the stitches on the ball, the spin, the tornado, all that stuff my dad told me.

I told Jim it's nearly impossible for a pitcher to throw a fastball and a curve with the same motion. Most pitchers "telegraph" when they're throwing the curve. Maybe their delivery is a little different, or their arm speed is slower. But if you watch carefully, you'll know when the curve is coming. Sometimes you can see the pitcher twist his wrist as he releases the ball.

I taught Jim how to read the spin of the ball. A fastball has backspin because it tumbles off the pitcher's fingertips as they come straight down. So the seams spin *up*. With a curve, the ball spins sideways, and if you watch carefully you can see the seams as they spin. I taught him some other stuff too.

"Nobody ever told me that," Jim said when I

finished my little lesson. "Thank you kindly. I'll try that next time."

"Let us help you back to your hotel," Bobby said.

"I can manage," said Jim, as he started walking away slowly. "So long, boys. And thanks again."

"Are you sure you're gonna be okay?" I asked.

"A good sleep cures all ills," Jim said. "And I sleep like a log. Tomorrow's another day."

19

I Can Dig It

BOBBY AND I WATCHED AS JIM WALKED DOWN EIGHTH Avenue. He moved slowly, but he wasn't falling-down drunk or anything. He seemed okay. I was no longer worried that he might be a danger to himself or anybody else.

It was getting late. Time for us to go. I was tired, hungry, and hadn't used the bathroom in almost a hundred years. I pulled my new pack of baseball cards out of my pocket.

That's when two of the guys who were playing touch football on the field walked over to us. I hid my cards.

"Hey, we gotta go home for dinner," one of them said. "You guys wanna play?"

I looked up at the other four guys still on the field. They were waving their arms for us to come over.

"Thanks, but—" I said.

"You bet!" Bobby said, and he waved back to the guys.

I hate when he does that! I didn't want to play. I don't even like football, and the last time we played together, I had demonstrated pretty conclusively how terrible I am at the game. But Bobby didn't care. He started jogging over without even looking back.

I could have let him go. I *should* have let him go and just gone home by myself. That would show him. I could just leave him in 1913 and never have to deal with him again.

But I couldn't do that. Being the dope that I am, I put my baseball cards back in my pocket and followed him.

"Do we really need to do this?" I asked angrily. "I want to go home. I gotta go to the bathroom."

"Just hold it a little while, Stoshack," Bobby replied. "Have some fun for once in your life."

We went over to the boys on the field and introduced ourselves. They told us their names, which I forgot instantly. Short attention span, I guess.

But these guys were easy to remember, because one of them was really tall, one was kind of short, one was fat, and the fourth one had blond hair. I *did* remember that last guy's name, because his friends called him Blondie.

It seemed that Tall, Short, and Fat were on one team. The two guys who had to go home had been on the team with Blondie. Me and Bobby were invited to take their places, and Bobby quickly agreed. Tall seemed to be the leader, and he showed us the trees on either end of the field that they were using as goal lines.

"You guys kick off," Bobby said.

"Fine," Tall said. "Say, do you want to make it interesting?"

"Sure," said Bobby.

"What do you mean, make it interesting?" I asked.

Bobby pulled me aside.

"Moron," he said, "when somebody asks if you want to make it interesting, it means they want to bet on the game."

"Bet money?" I asked.

"No, idiot. Bet Popsicle sticks. Of *course* bet money!"

"How about a buck per man?" Short suggested as he and his teammates dropped back to kick off to us.

"Sure," Bobby agreed. "A buck it is."

"All we have is the 20 cents the groundskeeper gave us!" I whispered to Bobby. "If we lose, we won't be able to pay, and those guys will probably beat the crap out of us."

"You worry too much, Stoshack," Bobby whispered back. "Look at that fat guy and that shrimp. You think they're gonna beat us? The only money that matters is theirs, 'cause we're gonna take it."

"You *know* I can't play," I reminded him.

"Just do what I tell you," Bobby said, "and the money's in the bank."

Man, I wish I had that kind of confidence. Or maybe he was just stupid. Anyway, the other team kicked off and Bobby caught the ball on one bounce. It was a little wider than the footballs in our time, but the same length.

Bobby lateraled the ball to Blondie, who ran a few yards upfield. Just before he was about to get tagged, he lateraled it to me. I was cornered and got tagged before advancing the ball a yard.

I could describe every play of the game in detail for you, but it would be boring. Basically, Bobby and Blondie did the heavy lifting for our team. Blondie was our quarterback, and he had a good arm. Bobby caught most of the passes for us. I was holding my own. I blocked a few passes. I didn't make any spectacular plays, but nobody burned me or made me look dumb either.

After we had played for half an hour or so, there was no score. Even so, the game was interesting enough, in my opinion, without having to put money on it. Especially money we didn't have.

It was starting to get dark and I really had to go to the bathroom *bad*. When Blondie suggested we call it a game as soon as somebody scored, I was thrilled.

It was our ball, and we huddled up.

"Okay, what do you wanna do?" Bobby asked Blondie. I wasn't even part of the discussion, as they had already established the fact that I totally sucked and should have no say in the matter.

We had tried all the standard passing and running plays. They weren't fooling anybody.

"We need something different," Blondie said.

"Hey, you wanna try the Dig?" Bobby suggested.

"Oh no," I said. "Not the Dig." I remembered that goofball play Jim Thorpe told us about.

"The Dig?" Blondie asked. "What's the Dig?"

"It's a trick play," Bobby whispered. "Oldest trick in the book. They'll never know what hit 'em."

Bobby explained the Dig to Blondie and he nodded his head excitedly. They both agreed that because the other team was covering Bobby more carefully than me, it would make sense for me to be the digger and he would be the ultimate receiver.

We broke from the huddle. Bobby and I lined up on the left side and I hiked the ball to Blondie. I ran out about 15 yards, stopped, and turned around. Bobby ran deeper, maybe 10 yards or so past me.

"Hit me!" Bobby screamed. "I'm open!"

But he was just a decoy. Blondie threw the ball to me instead, just like we had planned. It was a perfect pass, chest high. As the ball flew toward me, I could sense the two defenders running over to tag me as soon as I made the catch.

I didn't catch the ball, though. I wasn't *supposed* to catch it. Instead, I put both hands under the ball, like you do when you're playing volleyball, and I tapped it up high into the air, over my head and backward. I had no idea where the ball was going to land. The two guys tagged me, but I didn't have the ball.

After hovering up in the air for a few seconds, it landed, of course, right in Bobby's hands. The guy who was supposed to be covering Bobby had switched to covering me as soon as he saw the pass heading in my direction. So when Bobby caught the ball, nobody was covering him. He ran the length of the field untouched.

"Oh yeah!" Bobby screamed. "*That's* what I'm talkin' about! Touchdown! We win! In your face! You owe each of us a dollar!"

He spiked the ball and did a touchdown dance like those receivers do on TV. The guys on the other team looked at him like he was crazy. I guess the end-zone celebration hadn't been invented yet in 1913.

"You can't do that!" Tall shouted.

"Why not?" Bobby asked.

"It's against the rules," insisted Fat.

"It was a forward lateral," said Short.

"No it wasn't," Bobby explained. "Stoshack never had possession of the ball. He just tipped it up in the air and I happened to be there to grab it."

"Yeah, I tipped it," I agreed.

They couldn't argue. Bobby was right. It was a devious play, and a little underhanded—in more ways than one. But there was nothing illegal about it.

"One dollar for each of us," Bobby said, holding

out his hand. "Cash only, please. We don't accept credit cards or any other kind of lame money you use here."

They looked like they wanted to kill us, but a bet is a bet. Tall, Short, and Fat managed to come up with the money. It occurred to me that three dollars probably seemed like a lot more money in 1913. Instead of just handing it over, Tall threw some bills and coins at Bobby's feet.

"You guys cheated," he said.

"Sour grapes," Bobby said as he gathered up the cash. He gave a dollar to Blondie, who thanked us and ran off. Tall, Short, and Fat stomped away, muttering to themselves.

"I *told* you we'd beat those guys!" Bobby said as soon as they were out of earshot.

"Let's go home," I said. "I gotta pee bad."

"Y'know, I was thinking," Bobby said. "We oughta give this money to Jim. We never woulda won it without him. It's the right thing to do."

"Since when do *you* do the right thing?" I asked.

"Come on, Stoshack. He needs it more than we do."

I had to admit he was right. Jim was broke. Besides, we probably couldn't spend the old money in the twenty-first century. And I could use the bathroom at Jim's place.

We walked a couple of blocks down Eighth Avenue until I spotted a sign for the Trinity Hotel. It didn't look like a very fancy place. In fact, the lobby looked a little dumpy. It was the kind of hotel you wouldn't want to stay in if you were on vacation.

There was one of those little bells on the front desk. I love ringing those things. Bobby tapped it and soon a guy appeared.

"May I help you gentlemen?" he asked.

"Can you please tell us Mr. Thorpe's room number?" Bobby asked in his polite, suck-up-to-adults voice. "I'm a long-lost relative."

"Yeah, *really* long lost," I added. Bobby stomped on my foot.

The guy looked at us over his glasses. For all I knew, autograph hounds showed up at the hotel all the time and he was about to call security to kick us out.

"Room 413," the guy said. "You rock, dude," Bobby replied, and the guy just stared at him.

There was no elevator. We found the steps up to the fourth floor. Room 413 was at the end of the hall.

Bobby knocked on the door softly. When nobody answered, he knocked harder. Still no answer. Finally, he twisted the doorknob to see if it would turn, and the door opened a crack.

"We shouldn't just walk in," I said.

"Come on," Bobby said, pushing the door open.

The front room was a mess. Paint was peeling from the walls. Boxes were scattered around, like Jim hadn't fully unpacked yet. But leaning against the walls were photos of him playing football and competing in the Olympics. Jim in his glory days.

**Pictures of Jim in his glory days
were leaning against the walls.**

"It's hot in here," Bobby said. "We should turn on the air conditioner."

"Sure," I said, "as soon as they invent it. I don't think Jim's here."

"He's gotta be here."

The place was pretty big for a hotel. There was a living room, a dining room, and a kitchen with just a stove and a sink. No dishwasher or refrigerator.

There was a door leading off the living room, and Bobby put his hand on the knob.

"Don't open it!" I said. "That must be Jim's bedroom."

"Then that must be where he *is*, Stoshack!" Bobby said, and he opened the door.

Jim was lying on the bed, facedown.

20

The Right Thing to Do

JIM LOOKED LIKE HE MIGHT BE DEAD. HIS FACE WAS buried in the pillow and his arm hung off the side of the bed. He was so still.

"Is he alive?" I asked Bobby.

"Relax, Stoshack," Bobby replied. "Can't you see him breathing? He went on a bender and he's sleeping it off. Didn't you ever get drunk?"

"No, I didn't."

It didn't surprise me to hear that Bobby had been drunk before. If he was addicted to something as dangerous as heroin, he *must* have used alcohol. Me, I took a sip of my dad's beer once and almost threw up. I don't know how anybody can drink that stuff.

Suddenly, Jim started mumbling in his sleep. It was hard to understand what he was saying. It sounded like, "I miss you, Charlie"—or something like that.

"Who's Charlie?" Bobby whispered.

"Beats me."

"I won those medals, Charlie," Jim mumbled. "Won 'em fair and square. You believe me, don't you?"

Jim rolled over and thrashed around, muttering something unintelligible.

"We can leave the money on the night table with a note," Bobby said.

"I gotta use the can first," I told Bobby.

I found my way to the bathroom, and was happy to see it had a regular toilet that flushed.

While I was doing my business, it occurred to me that since we'd been in 1913, Bobby hardly had any opportunity to use the syringe he was hiding in his backpack. That movie they showed us at school said junkies had to get a fix every few hours.

Right now would be the perfect time for him to shoot up, I realized. *Jim was asleep. I was in the bathroom. Bobby was alone.*

Flushing the toilet would tell him I was finished. Instead, I tiptoed out of the bathroom, sneaking back down the hall into Jim's bedroom. I fully expected to see Bobby with the syringe in his hand.

Well, he had the syringe in his hand all right. But he wasn't injecting himself with it.

He was about to stick it into *Jim!*

"What are you doing?!" I demanded.

"*Shhhhh!*" Bobby whispered. "You'll wake him."

"What are you doing?!" I repeated.

"None of your business."

Now, I don't know anything about wrestling, but I remembered the move Jim did on that big guy, Tesreau, in the Giants' locker room. I grabbed Bobby from behind, crossing one of my legs over his leg. Then I yanked up his hand that was holding the syringe and twisted the other one behind his back.

"Let *go* of me, Stoshack!" Bobby begged. "This is very dangerous!"

"I know," I grunted. "That's why I'm doing it. Drop the syringe."

Bobby tried one last time to break the hold, but I had him locked up.

"I call this the Armbreaker," I said.

"Okay, okay," he said, letting the syringe fall to the floor.

Jim, amazingly, slept through the whole thing. He really *did* sleep like a log.

"I can't *believe* this," I whispered. "You're trying to shoot him up with heroin?"

Bobby looked at me like I was nuts.

"Heroin?" he said. "I wasn't giving him heroin. Why would I do a crazy thing like that?"

"Because you're addicted," I said. "You're a junkie."

"Are you nuts?! What makes you think I'm a junkie?"

"You didn't want me looking in your backpack," I explained, "so I went in there while you were asleep outside the Polo Grounds. You had the syringe and two unmarked bottles."

"It's not heroin, you moron!" Bobby said.

"Then what *is* it?"

Bobby took a few seconds, then sighed.

"It's steroids," he said.

Steroids?!

In case you don't know, steroids are these really powerful drugs that some athletes use to build muscles. Steroids are banned in just about all sports. Some players have gotten caught using them and were fined, suspended, or even banned for years. It has become a huge issue in cycling, track, football, and baseball.

The fact that Bobby wanted to give Jim steroids floored me. I had been dead wrong. Bobby wasn't a junkie. He was a pusher! And he was pushing steroids!

"Where did you get that stuff?" I asked.

"A guy I know on the high-school football team takes 'em," Bobby said. "He sold me some."

"Are you out of your mind?" I asked him. "Steroids are dangerous! You don't know what the side effects might be! You probably don't even know how much to give him. He could have an overdose!"

"Will you lighten up, Stoshack?" Bobby said, his eyes flashing with anger. "Lots of athletes take steroids. It's not that big of a deal. And think about it. *Nobody* has them here. They haven't been invented yet. Jim Thorpe is the greatest athlete in the world. If he was the only guy in his time who had steroids, he would be better than Ruth, Aaron, DiMaggio—all of them put together! We would go back home and find the record books rewritten. Most home runs: Jim Thorpe. Most RBIs: Jim Thorpe. Highest slugging average—"

"That's insane!" I shouted. "You think injecting something into him is going to help him hit a curveball? He's a great athlete, but he's just not a great baseball player. That's all there is to it. Steroids *aren't* going to make him great."

"Wouldn't hurt," Bobby said.

Suddenly it all made sense to me. I relaxed my grip on Bobby. Now I knew the *real* reason he had showed up at my door that day.

"So *that's* why you wanted to go back in time!" I said. "You didn't want to meet your great-grandfather. You didn't want to help him get his medals back. You just wanted to shoot him full of drugs and turn him into some pumped-up muscle freak who would rewrite the record books!"

"What's so wrong with that?" Bobby protested. "Y'know, *you* gave me the idea, Stoshack. You said that coming here was my chance to right a wrong, remember? You said not many people ever have the power to do that. Well, I'm doing it. I think giving Jim steroids is the right thing to do."

Suddenly, Bobby reached down and grabbed the syringe off the floor. He was about to jab it into Jim.

So I slugged him. Right in the jaw.

"Owww!" Bobby yelled as he fell over. The syringe sailed across the room. Bobby landed right on top of Jim, who bolted up from his bed. He looked like he had seen a ghost.

"Wh—what are you kids doing here?" he demanded.

Jim couldn't possibly understand what steroids were. This was a man who had never seen television, never surfed the web, never heard of DNA or atomic bombs or space travel.

"Mr. Thorpe," I said before Bobby could get a word in. "We're really sorry. We thought we might be able to do something that would prevent you from losing. But we messed up."

"Here," Bobby said, pulling the bills and coins out of his pocket. "We won this from those guys playing football in the park. We pulled the Dig on them, and it worked."

"Take it," I said. "Your bartender says you owe him money."

"Thanks, boys," Jim said, accepting the cash.

Before we left, I wanted to ask him one question that had been on my mind ever since I'd talked to my dad.

"After the Olympics, why didn't you just cash in and get rich?" I asked. "You could have been a millionaire. Why did you go back to college and play football for free?"

"The team needed me," he said simply.

It was just a different time, I guess. I couldn't imagine anyone in the twenty-first century giving up the chance to make gobs of money. I hear about athletes who already earn ten million dollars a year, and as soon as their contract is up they jump to the first team that offers them eleven million. There's no loyalty anymore. Or maybe there never was. Maybe Jim Thorpe was just a really good guy.

"Jim," Bobby asked. "Who's Charlie? You were talking in your sleep to somebody named Charlie."

Jim grimaced and picked up a picture of two little boys from his night table.

"Charlie was my twin brother," he said.

"You have a twin?" I asked.

"He was my best friend too," Jim said. "But Charlie died when we were ten. Typhoid."

"I'm sorry," I said, as Jim buried his face in his hands.

While Jim wept and Bobby comforted him, I took the opportunity to retrieve the syringe and bottles and bring them down the hall to the bathroom. I squirted the liquid inside the syringe down the sink and poured out the contents of the two bottles. Jim didn't need steroids. Nobody needed steroids. Bobby Fuller could be so stupid sometimes.

When I got back from the bathroom, Bobby and Jim were sitting on the bed next to each other. Jim was listening to Bobby's iPod. His eyes were closed and he was bobbing his head up and down with the music.

Bobby's eyes were closed too. In one hand, he was holding a baseball card. In the other, he was holding Jim's hand.

21

Good and Bad

BOBBY FULLER HAS DONE SOME TERRIBLE THINGS TO ME over the years. But this was the ultimate. I couldn't believe he would try to leave me behind. That kid simply had no morals. No sense of right or wrong. No conscience. I could hardly believe what I was seeing.

"What are you doing?" I demanded.

"Nothing," Bobby said, letting go of Jim's hand. "Jim's rocking out."

I saw Bobby slip the baseball card behind his back. I reached into my pocket for my new pack of cards. It was there, but it had been opened.

"You're trying to take Jim home with you," I accused him, "and leave me here!"

"That's ridiculous, Stoshack," Bobby claimed. "I was just showing him how we do it."

"We?" I said. "*We? I'm* the one who has the power!

The power isn't in the *card*, you dope! The power is in *me*. You can't use it by yourself."

"I know that," he said. "We weren't going anywhere. We were just fooling around."

Jim's eyes were still closed. He was nodding his head to the music. He couldn't hear us.

"So you're a pickpocket too," I told Bobby.

"I am not," he replied. "I . . . found it."

I used to be a pretty emotional guy. I used to throw tantrums and lose my temper when somebody got me mad. I had to learn to keep my anger in check.

But this was the last straw. I'd had it with Bobby Fuller.

So I just jumped on him and started punching. I got a few good shots in before Jim realized what was going on.

"Knock it off!" he said, taking out the earbuds. "I thought you boys were friends."

"He was *never* my friend!" I yelled.

I don't think I've ever been so mad in my life. I was punching Bobby in the face and he was punching me back. It was the way little kids fight. No defense, all offense. I wasn't about to let up. I wanted to inflict more pain on Bobby than he was giving me.

Suddenly, Jim's huge hand grabbed the back of my shirt, pulling me and Bobby apart. I was panting like a dog. Bobby was too. I would have kept fighting anyway, but Jim wouldn't let go of us. He just held us like that until we calmed down.

"Say you're sorry," Jim ordered.

Bobby and I made some weak apologies to each other and Jim let us go.

"Stoshack," Bobby said, "think it over. We should take Jim home with us to Louisville! It would be great!"

"What would be so great about it?" I asked, still angry at him.

"Jim would be a superstar if he lived in the twenty-first century," said Bobby. "Nobody would care that he played baseball before the Olympics. He could make millions of dollars and live in a giant mansion and drive around in a Corvette or whatever car he wanted. Just imagine! They'd be making Jim Thorpe posters and Jim Thorpe bobble heads. He'd be dating supermodels and doing commercials for Coke and McDonald's and—"

"What's a bobble head?" Jim asked.

"It's a little statue that . . . oh, never mind," Bobby told him. "You like my iPod? Wait until you see an IMAX movie! We have satellite radio and high-definition TV too!"

"Jim doesn't know what you're talking about," I told Bobby. "They don't even have *regular* TV or radio here."

"So what?" Bobby said. "He would *love* the future."

"Could you really take me with you?" Jim asked. He looked like he actually wanted to come.

Nobody had ever wanted to before. I met Shoeless Joe Jackson just before he was about to be kicked out of baseball forever. It was all over for him. His life was ruined. He was disgraced. But when I offered to take him home with me, he said no. He wanted to stay in his own time, no matter how terrible it was.

And who could blame him? If some stranger from the next century came and offered to take me away from the world I knew, I'd probably tell him to buzz off.

"You want us to take you to the twenty-first century?" I asked.

"Maybe I wasn't meant for my time," Jim said. "Maybe I . . . maybe I was born too soon."

It never occurred to me that somebody could be born too early or too late for the time they live in. But I suppose a person might not fit into their time period, just like we might not fit into a shirt or a certain social group.

It made me think of Josh Gibson. He was very possibly the greatest power hitter in baseball history. They said he hit 800 home runs in the Negro Leagues. Josh died when he was thirty-five, just ten weeks before Jackie Robinson broke the color barrier. If he had been born ten years later, he might have been as famous as Babe Ruth. Maybe even *more* famous.

Jim was looking at me with pleading eyes. I weighed the pros and cons of bringing him home with us. The pros were obvious. We could make him a superstar. He was a natural athlete. With a smart hitting coach and a patient manager, he might become as good as any baseball player in the world. In the twenty-first century, he would be Michael Jordan, Tiger Woods, and Lance Armstrong all rolled into one.

But there were some cons too. What if Jim couldn't handle the shock of living in modern times? Going from a Model T to a Corvette might be too much for him.

For another thing, I've never taken *two* people with me before. It might not work. Maybe there's a limit, like when you fly on an airplane and they only let you take a certain number of suitcases. What if our bodies get ripped apart in the time-travel process?

"I can't do it," I finally decided. "If anything went wrong, I'd be responsible. It wouldn't be right to play with Jim's life."

"Stoshack," Bobby argued, "the whole reason we came here was to play with Jim's life! If we had kept him out of the Olympics, *that* would have changed everything for him."

He had a point. There was no big difference between changing Jim's life in 1913 or changing his life by taking him away from 1913.

"Excuse me," Jim said. He looked at Bobby. "You said you're my great-grandson. Is that the truth?"

"Yes," said Bobby.

"Well, if I went with you boys to your time," Jim said thoughtfully, "I wouldn't *have* any great-grandchildren there, would I? I wouldn't have any great-grandchildren at all."

He was right. It was the same reasoning behind our decision to stop Jim from committing suicide. If Jim died *or* if he came with us, he wouldn't get married and have children in his own time. His children obviously wouldn't have children either, so Bobby Fuller would never be born. Jim and I would return to the twenty-first century and Bobby would simply not exist.

"It's your decision, Bobby," I said.

I could see he was thinking it over. Bobby could sacrifice his own life to save Jim's reputation. Or, he could just save his own skin and leave Jim behind. Honestly, I'm not sure which I would choose if I was in his position. I wouldn't want to be in his shoes.

But Bobby never had to make the decision.

"I'm not going," Jim said. "I refuse to ruin someone else's life just so I can make mine better."

It didn't look like he was going to change his mind, so Bobby and I got up to leave. We said goodbye and told Jim we were sorry for the trouble we had caused him. He shook my hand and then held Bobby's for a long time.

"My great-grandson, there's an old Indian saying," Jim told him. "Bad in good and good in bad. All men have good in them. Let the good show itself."

"I will," Bobby said. "Is there anything I can do

for you before we go?"

"Yeah," Jim said. "Can I have that pod thing?"

Oooooooooh, iPods are expensive. Bobby probably saved up for a long time to buy his. And there would be no way for Jim to charge it up once the battery ran out. He would only get a few hours of music out of it.

"Sure," Bobby said, handing him the iPod.

We took the stairs down to the lobby and turned right onto Eighth Avenue. It was nighttime. The streets were empty. Most of the stores were closed for the day. I figured we would go back to the park and find a quiet spot where Bobby and I could relax and send ourselves home.

But we hadn't gotten more than 20 feet from the hotel when a hand clapped over my mouth. Another hand grabbed me around the chest.

Somebody was pulling me into an alley.

22

The Perfect Crime

"MAKE A SOUND AND WE'LL KILL YOU!" SAID THE GUY who grabbed me. Ugh, his breath stunk.

"Let go of me!" said Bobby.

I looked to my right and saw that Bobby had been grabbed by another guy. It was hard to see in the dim light, but I recognized the guy holding Bobby. He was Fat, one of the guys we had beaten in the football game before we went to Jim's hotel. The two of them must have been waiting for us the whole time we were upstairs with Jim.

"You guys cheated," said the one who was holding me. He must have been Tall, because he sure wasn't Short. "We want our money back."

"We don't have your money," Bobby told them, struggling to get free. "We gave it away."

"That's a lie!" said Fat.

I didn't know if these guys had weapons or not. I

also didn't know what they were planning to do with us if we couldn't come up with any cash. But there was one thing I knew for sure—I wasn't going to let them go through my pockets looking for it. If they found my baseball cards and decided to take them, that would be the end of us. Bobby and I would be stuck in the past forever.

Frantically, I looked around for something I could use to get free. The only thing in the alley was a bunch of garbage cans that were lined up a few feet to our left. The old metal kind. They would have to do.

Tall was already pulling me from behind. I had to take the risk that he didn't have a gun or a knife. I leaned back so I was pushing hard against him. Then I rammed him into the garbage cans.

"Hey!" was all he managed to say before the two of us fell over backward. His body took the brunt of it, slamming into the cans with the added weight of me on top of him. Tall also cushioned my fall, and in the process of crashing into the cans, he let go of me.

I don't know how Bobby got free, but when I jumped up, he was holding a garbage can over his head. Fat was on the ground below him. Bobby slammed the can down on Fat. Then he picked up another can. I thought he was going to hit Fat or Tall with it, but instead he tilted it and dumped the garbage over their heads. Nice touch. And they didn't have Hefty bags in 1913. It was disgusting.

"Run!" I yelled, and we tore out of the alley onto Eighth Avenue.

"Let's get 'em!" I heard one of them shout behind us.

"Split up!" Bobby yelled when we reached the corner. "It'll make it harder for them to find us."

I ran down the street and into the park where we had been playing football. There were lots of good hiding places in there. I hoped Bobby had the same idea. We would be hard to find in the dark.

The problem was, it was hard to find those hiding places because the streets were lit with these dinky little gas lamps and I couldn't see five feet in front of me. I found that out the hard way when I tripped and almost took a header over a tree root. I decided it would be safer to hide behind a bush and wait there until Fat and Tall got tired of hunting for us.

I was sweating, and I could feel my heart pounding. There was some shouting in the distance, but it didn't sound like Fat and Tall were heading in my direction. It sounded like they were running down the street. I wondered where Bobby was.

As I crouched there in the dark, I checked my pocket for my pack of baseball cards. Got 'em.

It would be so easy, I thought as I took out one of the cards. I could get out of here. I could go back home, and be safe. I wouldn't have to worry about those guys chasing us. And I wouldn't have to worry about Bobby Fuller ever again, because I could just leave him in 1913.

Would that be so horrible to do? I mean, he was going to do the same thing to *me*. He just couldn't. But I *could*. What would be so wrong with leaving him behind?

I started feeling the faintest tingling sensation in my fingertips.

I tried to imagine what would happen if I left Bobby behind. I would get home and Bobby Fuller simply wouldn't exist anymore. He could never bother me again. He could never bother *anybody* again. Maybe I would be doing the world a service. I could even be saving lives, if Bobby were to grow up to become a murderer or a dangerous criminal.

The tingling sensation in my fingers started getting stronger. It was moving up my arm.

If I left Bobby behind, nobody would ever know what had happened to him. The police would search all over Louisville, with dogs. They might question me, because I was the last person who had seen him before his disappearance. Maybe they'd bring in one of those psychic detectives you see on TV. There would be newspaper articles, flyers stapled to telephone poles around town, and pictures of Bobby on milk cartons.

But eventually the police would have to give up. They'd never find a body or any evidence of wrongdoing. They'd have to conclude that Bobby Fuller had just vanished. It would be the perfect crime.

I dropped the card.

What was I, crazy? What kind of a monster had I

become? I was seriously thinking about doing away with someone!

Just because Bobby would be willing to leave *me* behind didn't mean it would be okay for me to leave *him* behind. If I lowered myself to his level, I would be no better than he was.

"Bobby?" I called, quietly at first, and then a little louder. "Bobby!"

The park was silent. At least five minutes had passed since I'd last heard the voices of those guys who were chasing us. Either they were gone or they were hiding in the dark, waiting to grab me again.

"Over here," Bobby finally called.

I felt around in the dark until I found him about 50 feet away, hiding behind a tree.

"Are they gone?" I asked.

"I think so."

"Let's blow this pop stand."

"You got that right," Bobby replied.

Bobby and I found a comfortable spot on the grass under the tree. We were both anxious to go. He gave me the card he had stolen from me earlier and grabbed my hand. I closed my eyes, even though I could barely see anything with them open anyway. It didn't take long for the tingling sensation to come back and do its magic as it worked its way up my arm and across my body.

Soon I reached the point of no return. I felt our bodies disappearing.

We were gone.

23

Run on Anything

"JOEY! HURRY UP!"

The instant Bobby and I got back from 1913, my mom started yelling that I was late for my game. Bobby went home and Mom dropped me off at Dunn Field on her way to work. I was still buttoning up my jersey when I jumped out of the car.

"Stosh!" Flip Valentini shouted when he saw me. "Where *were* you? We needed you!"

"I'm sorry!" I said, but Flip and the guys on my team didn't look like they were ready to accept my apology. One glance at the scoreboard told me why. We were batting in the bottom of the last inning, and we were down by a run to the Exterminators. They no longer had Kyle the Mutant, but they were still good. There were two outs. The bases were empty. It was almost a hopeless situation.

"We really needed to *beat* these bums!" Flip

snapped when I got to the bench. "You let the team down, Stosh."

Phillip Rollison was walking up to the plate. He was batting fourth, which would have been my spot in the lineup.

"Can I pinch-hit?" I asked Flip. I really wanted to help the team, and I wanted to make up for being so late.

"Fuhgetaboutit," he barked. "That wouldn't be fair to the guys who showed up on time. You wanna help? Go coach third."

Phillip bounced to short on the first pitch, and it looked like that would end the game. But the shortstop bobbled the ball and Phillip was safe at first base. We had the tying run on with two outs.

Owen Jones grabbed his bat and we all knew what he had to do—advance Phillip to second so he would be in position to score on a single. The third baseman took a few steps toward home plate in case Owen was bunting, although that wasn't likely with two outs.

But that's exactly what he did. Owen squared around and dropped the ball down about three feet in front of the plate. Phillip took off for second base.

The Exterminators' catcher threw off his mask and pounced on the ball. He whipped it to first. You could tell he hurried his throw, and it was high. The first baseman jumped and reached for the ball, but it was over his head and into rightfield. Everybody started screaming.

"Keep going!" I shouted to Phillip as he rounded second. "Go!"

The rightfielder picked up the ball and threw it to second. That was a mistake. He should have thrown it home. Phillip had just about reached third.

I had a quick decision to make. Should I wave Phillip around third to try and score the tying run? Or should I tell him to hold up and hope the next batter could drive him in? Who was up next? I didn't know, and there was no time to turn my head away to find out. How fast was Phillip? What kind of an arm did the second baseman have? So many little decisions. All I had was a millisecond to decide what to do.

Sometimes you just have to gamble.

"GO!" I shouted to Phillip, windmilling my arm around.

Phillip rounded third and dug for the plate.

"Home it!" the Exterminators yelled, and the second baseman relayed the ball to the catcher, who was ready for the inevitable collision.

The ball bounced a few feet in front of the plate. When the catcher went to scoop up the short hop, Phillip came barreling in and knocked him over. Arms and legs, caps and gloves were flying. The ball skittered to the backstop. Phillip touched the plate with his hand.

"Safe!" yelled the ump.

Everybody on our bench and the parents in the

bleachers were going crazy. We had tied the game! Just as important, Owen had advanced all the way to third in the confusion. He had bunted for a triple. Good hustle!

The winning run was only 90 feet from home. I was afraid Flip was going to have a heart attack from all the excitement.

The pitcher was furious, stomping around the mound and glaring at his catcher. If he hadn't chucked the ball into the outfield, the game would have been over. The Exterminators' coach jogged out to the mound and whispered a few words to calm down his pitcher.

Carlos Montano was up next. He looked nervous. I knew he didn't like pressure situations, and the game was on the line. Nobody likes to make the last out in a game. You always feel like it's your fault. I should know.

Coaching third, I leaned over to whisper to Owen.

"Two outs," I reminded him. "Run on anything. A grounder. A hit. A fly ball. A wild pitch. *Anything.* Got it?"

"Run on anything," Owen repeated.

The Exterminators' pitcher looked in for the sign. That was when I got a brainstorm.

"Hey, pitcher!" I yelled.

The pitcher looked over at me.

"Lemme see that ball for a sec, will ya?" I asked.

"What for?"

"Just lemme see it," I said, holding my hands out to catch it.

He flipped me the ball underhanded. I stepped aside to let it roll past me.

"Go! Go! Go!" I shouted to Owen.

Owen took off and crossed home plate standing up, with the winning run.

Well, let me tell you, there has never been such a ruckus on a Little League field. The Exterminators' coach shot out of his dugout like it was filled with cockroaches. The pitcher was throwing a tantrum. Screaming parents came running off the bleachers, waving their arms around. I half expected the cops to show up and start dragging people off to jail.

"That's illegal!" the coach screamed at the umpire. "They can't do that!"

"There's nothing in the rule book that says you can't ask to see the ball," the ump explained. "Your pitcher threw it away."

The guys on our team were going nuts. We had finally beaten the Exterminators. Flip gave me a big hug and told me he was sorry he yelled at me. Everybody was clapping me on the back, as if I had driven in the winning run. And I hadn't even set foot on the field.

In the middle of all the celebrating, I felt a tap on my shoulder. I turned around and was more than a little surprised to see Bobby Fuller standing there.

In the mad rush after returning from 1913, we

hadn't had the chance to talk about our trip at all. After what we'd been through together, I was actually happy to see him.

"Nice move getting that runner home," he said with a smirk. "Hmmm, I wonder where you got that idea."

"Oldest trick in the book," I said.

"Did you hide some baseballs in the outfield grass too?" Bobby asked.

"Very funny."

"Y'know, there's hope for you, Stoshack," Bobby told me. "Maybe you're not such a Goody Two-shoes after all. With a little push, you could come over to the dark side with me."

"Doubtful," I replied. "Extremely doubtful."

While I was talking with Bobby, my dad came rolling over. Dad rarely comes to my games. He says it's because the field isn't wheelchair accessible, but I always thought there was more to it than that.

"Smart thinking, son," he said. "Did you come up with that all by yourself?"

"Believe it or not," I told him, "John McGraw taught it to me. In 1913."

"You did it?!" Dad said, all excited. "You met McGraw? What was he like? Was he the jerk they say he was? Did you get something signed for me?"

Oh, no! In all the excitement, I had completely forgotten to bring back something signed by John McGraw for my dad. I was kicking myself. Dad doesn't have a lot of pleasure in his life, and this would have given him some.

"Actually he did get something signed for you, Mr. Stoshack," Bobby said.

He reached into his backpack and pulled out a thin book. The title was *Rules of Baseball*. I remembered seeing that. It was the book John McGraw was reading in the Giants' dugout.

"What's this?" Dad asked.

"It's John McGraw's personal rule book," Bobby told my dad. "See, he wrote a bunch of comments in the margins, and he signed it too."

John J. McGraw.

"McGraw said he read the rules so he would know how to break them," I added.

My dad looked like he was holding a chunk of solid gold. I hadn't seen such a big smile on his face in a long time.

"John McGraw's personal rule book!" Dad marveled. "This is priceless! It's like owning Shoeless Joe Jackson's shoes." My dad thanked me, and said he would see me soon.

By that time, most everybody had cleared the field. Bobby and I were alone on the grass, just like we were when we snuck into the Polo Grounds.

"How'd you get McGraw's rule book?" I asked Bobby.

"How do you think?" he replied. "I'm a pick-pocket. Duh!"

"You are evil, man!" I said, but we both had a laugh over it.

There was an awkward pause after that. The field was awfully quiet. Bobby was still hanging around, which was kind of weird. We'd never been friends. I kept expecting him to say he had to go somewhere, but he didn't.

"Listen," Bobby finally said, "I never had the chance to thank you."

"Forget it," I told him. "It was cool for me to meet Jim Thorpe too."

"No, I mean I wanted to thank you for not leaving me behind back there, in 1913. You could have. I deserved it."

"I know," I said. "Don't think I didn't consider it."

"Part of me wishes you *had* left me there," Bobby said.

"Leave you in the past?! Why?"

"Y'know how Jim said he lived in the wrong time?" said Bobby. "Well, sometimes I feel the same way. I kinda liked it back in the bad old days."

"We can go back to visit sometime, if you want," I told him.

"I just might take you up on that," he said. Bobby put out his hand, and I shook it.

"There's still hope for you, man," I told him. "With a little push, you could come over to the light side with me."

"Doubtful, Stoshack," he said. "Extremely doubtful."

Well, all in all, things worked out okay. At least I didn't get shot at this time.

I guess Jim was right. There's bad in good and good in bad. I always thought I was a pretty good kid. But I had just cheated to win a ball game. And I had come within seconds of leaving Bobby in 1913—nearly making him vanish from the face of the earth.

Then there's Bobby, who I always thought was the baddest of the bad. I never told him I promised to bring back a souvenir for my dad. He could have kept John McGraw's rule book for himself, maybe sold it for thousands of dollars. But he gave it to my dad for nothing. And he gave Jim his iPod too. There was some good in him after all, just like there was some bad in me.

As I watched Bobby walk away, I realized something. Sometimes you can change history, and sometimes history can change you.

Facts and Fictions

EVERYTHING IN THIS BOOK IS TRUE, EXCEPT FOR THE stuff I made up. It's only fair to tell you which is which.

Jim Thorpe, John McGraw, Christy Mathewson, Lord Byron, and all the players of 1913 were real people. After Jim Thorpe's Olympic medals were taken away from him in January 1913, a number of major-league baseball teams made him offers. It's too bad he chose the New York Giants; he and John McGraw could not get along, and Jim never got the chance to develop as a baseball player. Jim was fast and had a great arm, but had problems at the plate. He got just 35 at bats in 1913, and he only made five hits (for an average of .143). The Giants won the pennant easily, but lost their third World Series in a row. Jim never got a World Series at bat. The next season, McGraw let him bat just 31 times and he got

185

six hits. In 1915, Jim got twelve hits in 52 at bats.

The rap on Jim was that he couldn't hit a curveball, as seen in this short piece that appeared in *The New York Times* on March 15, 1916:

JIM THORPE'S LAST CHANCE.

McGraw's Final Test of Indian as Batsman for Giants.

Jim Thorpe, the Sac and Fox Indian, Olympic prize winner, and one of the greatest football players that ever donned gridiron armor, is making his last stand on the major league baseball diamond. Without question one of the greatest athletes ever developed in America or in any other portion of the world, Thorpe has made a name for himself in track and field sports, lacrosse, football, and college baseball. It was not until he undertook to play the latter game in the big leagues that he found a sport wherein he failed to shine with his accustomed brilliance.

Fresh from his Olympic triumphs at Stockholm and the subsequent sensational stripping away of these honors by the Amateur Athletic Union on the charge that he was a professional, Thorpe was signed to play with the New York National League Club by Manager John J. McGraw. From the very beginning the redskin athlete ran like a deer in the outfield and on the bases, fielded well, but was absolutely helpless before the curved pitching of the big league box stars.

Given a straight ball across the heart of the plate, Thorpe with his powerful arms and shoulders could and did lift the ball over the centerfielder's head, with great regularity. The trouble was that the pitcher never made such a mistake but once. Thereafter Thorpe got nothing but curved pitching, and the Indian swung on the slants in vain.

McGraw eventually did get rid of Jim.

Interestingly, after Jim was traded, he started to hit. In 1919—his final year in the majors and the only season he was given a real chance (159 at-bats)—Jim hit .327 for the Boston Braves. So he must have hit at least a few curveballs (maybe because Stosh taught him how?). Jim's lifetime major-league average was a respectable .252. We'll never know how good he could have been if he had signed with a team that was more supportive from the start.

In 1915, while still playing baseball, Jim began to play professional football for the Canton Bulldogs. He played for other pro teams too, and when the American Professional Football Association was formed in 1920, Jim was hired to be its president. The APFA later became the NFL. Football was Jim Thorpe's true love.

Jim suffered from bad timing. The Depression struck soon after he retired from sports in 1928. He took whatever work he could find to support his growing family (seven children with three wives). He was a house painter, security guard, bartender, and bouncer, and he managed an Indian wrestler named Sunny War Cloud. Jim even had some small roles in movies, such as *Klondike Annie*, with Mae West, and *Northwest Passage*, with Spencer Tracy. And yes, in 1931, he *was* one of the laborers who helped build Los Angeles County Hospital.

Greatest Athlete Back To Job of Manual Labor

Back in 1912, the name of Jim Thorpe meant more to sport fans than the name of Ruth, Rockne, and Bobby Jones means today. Thorpe was king of the athletic realm. He had gone to Stockholm to

represent America in the Olympic games and all he did was win the pentathlon and decathlon by excelling the world's foremost athletes in 11 different events.

He was a good swimmer, a good skater, a fine oarsman. In football he was supreme. He was described in his prime as being able to run better, sidestep better, and plunge harder than any contemporary or any who had gone before him. He captained his team, the Carlisle Indians.

He played basket ball and played any position. In baseball he was equally at home in the outfield and infield, although he never made the grade as a big league player.

Thorpe was an international sport sensation at the height of his power, when after having won every medal, practically, at Stockholm, it was revealed that prior to this he had played professional baseball in the south. He still remained the world's greatest athlete, but he was shorn of his amateurism. He at first denied the charges, then confessed to his professionalism.

JIM THORPE.

Canton and Massillon people remember well his professional football activities after he had left Carlisle.

This one-time greatest star, and international figure, is shown here as a day laborer on a hospital site in Los Angeles. Kings once bowed to the Indian athletic marvel of all time, now a day laborer.

The story you just read took place just 23 years after the United States Army killed Sitting Bull and 153 Lakota Sioux at Wounded Knee, South Dakota. That was the end of the Indian Wars. Many people still considered Native Americans to be "savages" even after Jim Thorpe stunned the world at the

1912 Olympics. Few people know that Native Americans—the *original* Americans—were not even granted American citizenship until 1924.

Jim Thorpe was proud of his Indian heritage. Toward the end of his life, he started a new career as a public speaker, traveling the country to give lectures on behalf of Indian education, citizenship, and equal rights. Health problems eventually slowed him down. He died on March 28, 1953, after his third heart attack, in Long Beach, California. He had been living there in a trailer park.

Jim Thorpe had a hard life—and a hard death too. He was buried in Shawnee, Oklahoma, but when the town refused to build a memorial for him, Jim's wife Patsy moved his body to Tulsa. Plans for a memorial didn't work out there, either.

Patsy heard that the Pennsylvania towns of Mauch Chunk and East Mauch Chunk were thinking about merging and changing their names. She agreed for Jim to be buried there if they named the town in his honor. They did, and that's where Jim is buried today. Jim Thorpe never set foot in Jim Thorpe, Pennsylvania.

After his death, Jim began to get some long overdue recognition for his accomplishments. He is now a member of the College Football Hall of Fame, Pro Football Hall of Fame, National Track and Field Hall of Fame, United States Olympic Hall of Fame, Pennsylvania Hall of Fame, and National Indian

Hall of Fame. In 2000, when *ABC's Wide World of Sports* set out to name the Athlete of the Century, they didn't choose Michael Jordan, Babe Ruth, or Muhammad Ali. They chose Jim Thorpe over them all.

As a man, Jim was complicated. Having survived an abusive father, his twin brother's death, lifelong prejudice against Indians, the Olympic scandal, career failure, and the death of his own son from infantile paralysis, it's not surprising that he had problems with alcohol.

Jim was also a modest, generous, and kind man who actually would give money to strangers and lift up people's cars to help them change tires. When asked what was the greatest moment in his athletic career, he would invariably talk about a fish he once caught rather than his Olympic or football heroics.

Jim never fought to get his Olympic medals returned. But attitudes about professional athletes participating in the Olympics changed over the years, and there were many attempts by others to clear his name. In 1983, two of Jim's children were presented with reproductions of his gold medals. (The originals had been lost, stolen from museums.) In 1992, professional athletes were finally allowed to participate in the Olympics.

In 2001, Jim Thorpe was finally recognized as a true American hero: His picture was on a Wheaties box.

Much of what was described in 1913 really happened. Christy Mathewson really did play six games of checkers simultaneously. Guys were constantly challenging Jim Thorpe to fights and wrestling matches. Newspapers really did create telegraphic simulations of baseball games. There are only two known copies of the Colgan's Jim Thorpe card, making it one of the rarest cards in the world.

The Polo Grounds was virtually the capital of baseball in the first half of the twentieth century. After the Giants moved to San Francisco, it became home to the Mets for their first two seasons. It was torn down in the mid-sixties and replaced with an apartment building.

There are also some minor fibs, stretchers, and outright lies in this book. While John McGraw *did* attempt to pass off an African American named Charley Grant as Chief Tokahoma, it happened back in 1901. Similarly, while McGraw's groundskeeper was famous for sculpting the foul lines and bending the rules in every possible way, that was when he was with the Baltimore Orioles in the 1890s.

The 1931 Jim Thorpe baseball card is a fake that my wife, Nina, made. There was no 1931 Jim Thorpe baseball card.

That story about Jim hitting three homers in three states is a myth. But you'll see it over and over again in books about him.

There may very well have been a Trinity Hotel and an Eighth Avenue Saloon, but I don't know. I just made them up.

Finally, Stosh, Bobby, Flip, and all the current-day characters are fictional. Time travel is impossible . . . or at least we haven't figured out how to do it yet.

Read More!

WANT TO LEARN MORE ABOUT JIM THORPE? I GOT MOST OF the information from reading books like Bill Crawford's biography of Jim Thorpe (*All American: The Rise and Fall of Jim Thorpe*), Charles C. Alexander's biography of John McGraw (*John McGraw*), Ray Robinson's biography of Christy Mathewson (*Matty: An American Hero*), and Frank DeFord's *The Old Ball Game: How John McGraw, Christy Mathewson and the New York Giants Created Modern Baseball*. Also, Noel Hynd's *The Giants of the Polo Grounds: The Glorious Times of Baseball's New York Giants* and *Land of the Giants: New York's Polo Grounds* by Stew Thornley were helpful.

There are books about Jim Thorpe for children of all ages. You should be able to find some of these in your local library:

Bruchac, Joseph. *Jim Thorpe's Bright Path*. New York: Lee & Low, 2004.

Fall, Thomas. *Jim Thorpe*. New York: Crowell, 1970.

Hahn, James and Lynn. *THORPE! The Sports Career of James Thorpe*. Mankato, Minn.: Crestwood House, 1981.

Lipsyte, Robert. *Jim Thorpe: 20th Century Jock*. New York: HarperCollins, 1993.

Richards, Gregory B. *Jim Thorpe: World's Greatest Athlete*. Chicago: Children's Press, 1984.

Wheeler, Robert W. *Jim Thorpe: World's Greatest Athlete*. Norman, Okla: University of Oklahoma Press, 1979.

Permissions

The author would like to acknowledge the following for use of photographs: George Brace: 118; Carnegie Library, Pittsburgh: 117; Library of Congress: 21, 91, 98, 122; National Baseball Hall of Fame Library, Cooperstown, NY: 85, 90, 119, 129; Zach Rice: 55; Nina Wallace: 21, 26, 75, 186; Howard Wolf: 197.

About the Author

Jim & Me is Dan Gutman's eighth baseball card adventure. You might also want to read *Honus & Me, Jackie & Me, Babe & Me, Shoeless Joe & Me, Mickey & Me, Abner & Me,* and *Satch & Me*. Dan (seen here at the site of the Polo Grounds) is also the author of *The Get Rich Quick Club, Johnny Hangtime,* and the My Weird School series. You can find out more about Dan and his books at www.dangutman.com.

Don't miss the tenth
thrilling Baseball Card Adventure—

Roberto & Me

"STOSH, YOU ARE THE MAN!" BRIAN WENZEL YELLED FROM
our dugout. "The man with the plan!"

I stepped up to the plate and tapped my bat
against my spikes. It was the sixth inning, which is
the last inning in our league. One out. Joe Koch was
on first and Clay VanderMeeden was on second. A
double would tie it for us. A home run would win it.
I'm not a home run hitter. In a situation like this, a
single would make me very happy.

I looked over at our coach, Flip Valentini, to see
if maybe he wanted me to lay down a bunt to move
the runners over to second and third. I figured there
was a pretty good chance, because Flip knows I
haven't been hitting very well lately. I struck out in
the second inning, and in the fourth I hit a weak
grounder back to the pitcher. If I hit into a double
play right now, the game would be over.

But Flip wasn't looking at me. He was looking at the runners and touched his right arm to his left sleeve. *The steal sign.* Flip was telling Joe and Clay to attempt a double steal on the next pitch. Then he looked at me and touched his right ear. *The take sign.* He was telling me I shouldn't swing no matter what.

Okay, I get it. If I were to drop down a sacrifice bunt, we would give up an out to advance two runners into scoring position. But Joe and Clay are both pretty fast. If they pull off a double steal, we move both runners without giving up an out. So then we would have two chances to drive in the runners instead of one. Smart. Flip has been around forever. He's probably forgotten more about baseball in his life than I'll ever learn.

The pitcher looked in for his sign, and then he looked at Clay on second. He wound up and threw. Out of the corner of my eye, I saw Joe and Clay digging for second and third. The pitch was right down the middle. I probably could have hit it pretty hard. But when Flip tells me not to swing, I don't swing.

"Strike!" hollered the ump.

The catcher jumped up from his squat and fired the ball to third. Clay came sliding in with a cloud of dust. The throw was there. The third baseman only had to catch the ball and slap the tag on Clay's leg.

"Yer out!" hollered the ump.

Ouch! Two outs. Clay didn't argue the call. They had him by a foot. The catcher pointed his finger

2

toward third as if it was a gun and blew on it. *Jerk.* Joe advanced to second on the play.

I looked over at Flip, and he shrugged his shoulders. You win some; you lose some. Even smart strategy fails sometimes.

All I knew was that I could still tie the game. But I'd need a hit, and I hadn't had one in a while.

"C'mon, Stosh!" Flip yelled, clapping his hands. "It's all you, babe. All you."

"Drive me in, Stosh!" Joe shouted from second base.

I dug my cleats into the dirt of the batter's box. The pitcher looked in for the sign. He wheeled and delivered. It looked outside to me. I didn't swing.

"Strike!" hollered the ump.

Okay. That was borderline. Maybe it was a strike. Maybe not. Doesn't matter. Don't think about the past. Worry about the present and the future. Two strikes now. Gotta protect the plate. Swing at anything close. No way I'm gonna strike out looking.

I tried to remember all the advice people have given me over the years: *Relax. Keep your eye on the ball. Take a breath. Quick bat. Turn your hips. Bend your knees. Don't grip the bat too tightly. Take a practice swing. Focus.*

Too much to think about.

The pitcher was ready now, and so was I. He went into his windup and let it fly.

The pitch looked good, and I took a rip at it. I got a piece of the ball, but not a good piece. It went curving into foul territory down the first base line. The catcher and first baseman gave chase.

"Get out of here!" I yelled at the ball, trying to will it out of play.

The first baseman leaned against the fence and reached over into the first row of seats. It didn't look like he was going to get it, but I guess the ball was curving back, because it ended up at the top of the webbing of his glove. Part of the ball was showing. A snow cone, we call it.

Shoot! Nice catch, I had to admit.

"Three outs!" hollered the ump. "That's the ball game, fellows."

I cursed at myself and trudged back to the bench. Nobody wants to make the last out of a game. And nobody wants to make the last out on a lame pop foul.

"You'll get 'im next time, Stosh," Brian said.

What was I doing wrong? Maybe I was trying too hard. Maybe I wasn't trying hard enough. Who knew? There are so many things that can go wrong when you're hitting.

I remember reading in some book that the hardest thing to do in any sport is to hit a baseball. I mean, think about it. You're holding a round bat and you're trying to hit a round ball. That's not easy right there. Plus, a good fastball reaches the plate about a half second after the pitcher releases it. You have like two-tenths of a second to decide whether or not to swing. The ball could be coming at different speeds, from different locations. It could be a curveball. It could be out of the strike zone, making it hard to hit. Or it could be coming at your head. Even if you manage to hit the ball, if you hit it a fraction of an inch too low or too high, you're probably out. Or somebody in the field can make a great play and catch it. And sometimes you hit it right at somebody.

No wonder players who can get a hit just three times in ten at bats are considered superstars. It's a game of failure. You fail seven times out of ten and you're doing great.

I chucked my bat against the fence near our dugout in disgust.

"Hey, none of that, son!" the ump yelled at me.

I plopped down on the bench next to Coach Valentini, who was wiping his forehead with a handkerchief.

"I suck," I muttered to nobody in particular.

"You're in a slump," Flip said. "It happens to everybody, Stosh. Even the great ones—Cobb, Williams, DiMaggio, Aaron—they all had slumps. I remember this one time in 1954—"

Usually I enjoy listening to Flip tell his baseball stories about the good old days. But today, I just wasn't in the mood.

"What can I do to get out of my slump?" I asked him.

Flip has been playing and coaching baseball for something like seventy years. If anybody knew how to get out of a slump, I figured it would be Flip.

"Ah, the great mystery of life," he said. "Nothin' you *can* do. Fuhgetuhboutit. You just gotta wait it out, Stosh. Believe me, the hits will come. You're too good a hitter to stay in a slump for long."

He was trying to make me feel good. I didn't want to hear it.

I was packing up my equipment when I heard a buzz in the bleachers behind our bench. I turned around to check it out. It was a troop of Girl Scouts. They were marching through the crowd with cans. I figured they were selling cookies, but then I noticed one of them carrying a sign that said, SAVE THE POLAR BEARS.

"Oh, give me a break," said our third baseman, Ricky Hernandez.

"Hey, why don't you girls get a life?" said our catcher, Teddy Ronson, when the Girl Scouts got within earshot.

"Why don't you guys get a conscience?" said the girl holding the sign. "Do you realize that burning fossil fuels has warmed the atmosphere so much that Arctic sea ice is melting, making it harder for polar bears to hunt for food? In forty years, they all could be gone. Extinct."

"Boo-hoo. I'm crying," said Tommy Rose.

"Ya think that if humans were dying off, the bears would go around with cans collecting money for *us*?" said Lucas Riley.

"Hey, you girls should adopt the polar bears and turn them into pets," said Tommy.

We were all laughing. The guys started in making cracks about the Bad News Bears, the Care Bears, Smokey the Bear, and every other kind of bear they could think of.

I had to admit that I felt the same way. I've got enough problems of my own trying to hit the ball. I can't worry about a bunch of bears.

"What are you gonna do with that money you're collecting?" I asked. "Buy freezers for the polar bears?"

All the guys laughed and gave me high fives, which made me feel good. At the same time I felt a little guilty. I've got nothing against polar bears. I just don't like fouling out with the tying run on second to end the game.

2

A Mission of Mercy

AS I PEDALED MY BIKE HOME, I MANAGED TO GET MY MIND off the game by thinking about my birthday. It was coming up, and I decided to ask for a portable video game system. I have a secondhand Game Boy that is like a thousand years old. But I saw in a magazine that Nintendo has a new system coming out that is very cool.

I hopped my bike over the edge of the driveway and wheeled it into the garage. In the kitchen, my mom was preparing dinner, still in her nurse's uniform. She works in the emergency room at Louisville Hospital. Usually she works the night shift, but today she was home early.

"Hey, Mom, I was thinking," I started, "for my birthday—"

I probably should have checked her mood before launching into the conversation.

"Mister, you're in trouble," she told me.

She didn't have to tell me I was in trouble. I knew I was in trouble because the only time my mother ever calls me "mister" is when I'm in trouble.

She handed me a piece of paper that said PROGRESS REPORT at the top. In between report cards, my school sends out progress reports to parents to let them know if their kid is screwing up or not. I don't know why they call it a progress report if they basically say you're not making much progress.

The progress report said that I was doing fine in all my classes except Spanish. There was a note that said POOR WORK and some code after that.

"I thought I was doing okay in Spanish," I said.

"If flunking is okay," my mom said, "you were right. It says that if you don't do something to bring up your grade, Joey, you're going to get an F on your next report card."

I'm a pretty decent student. Let me say that right now. But I would be the first to admit that I'm not very good in Spanish. I just don't get it. I don't see why I have to learn a foreign language, anyway.

At my school, we have to take Spanish, German, French, and Italian, each for one marking period. Then, at the end of the term, we choose one language to study the following year. I'm definitely *not* going to choose Spanish.

The next day, like it or not, I had to go talk to my teacher, Señorita Molina, to see what I could do to bring up my grade. I have Spanish last period on Thursdays, so I just waited until the other kids left the class before approaching Señorita Molina.

She's an okay lady, I guess. Kids think she's kind of strange. Like, she keeps a lit candle on her desk at all times, but she never tells anybody why.

Señorita Molina can't walk. She's in a wheelchair, and the whiteboard in her classroom is lower than normal so she can write on it from a sitting position. There have been lots of times in the lunchroom when me and some other kids sit around and try to guess what happened to Señorita Molina to make her disabled. But nobody knows for sure. And nobody has the nerve to ask her. She's one of those teachers who gives you the impression she doesn't want to talk about personal stuff.

"*Buenos dias, Tito,*" she said when I came over to her desk.

Tito is my Spanish name. On the first day of school, Señorita Molina said that each of us had to choose a Spanish name for ourselves. Most of the names sounded lame, but Tito sounded kind of cool, so I chose it.

"My mom got the progress report in the mail," I said.

"I was disappointed, Tito," said Señorita Molina.

"I'll try harder," I told her.

"Tell you what," she said. "You can do an extra credit project to bring up that grade."

"What sort of extra credit project?" I asked.

"Whatever you like," she said. *"Usa tu imaginacióón, Tito.* Use your imagination."

She looked down at her papers, so I figured she was finished with me. I was about to leave; but then I figured, what the heck? Nobody else was around. It was just the two of us. What did I have to lose?

"Señorita Molina," I said, "why do you keep a candle burning on your desk?"

She looked up at me, not with anger in her eyes but with sorrow. She paused for a moment, as if she wasn't sure she wanted to confide in me or not.

"It is for Roberto Clemente," she finally said.

Well, being a big baseball fan, I knew a thing or two about Roberto Clemente. Just about the only thing I ever read is baseball books. I've got a whole shelf of them at home. I know a lot about baseball history, both from reading and from seeing it with my own eyes.

I knew that Roberto Clemente played for the Pittsburgh Pirates, mostly in the 1960s. Rightfield. He had a great arm, and he was one of the few players to reach 3,000 hits. No more, no less. 3,000 hits exactly. He's in the Baseball Hall of Fame.

Señorita Molina reached into her drawer and pulled out a framed picture.

"I met Mr. Clemente when I was *una ninita*, a very little girl," she told me. "I grew up in Puerto Rico, and so did he."

"How did you meet him?" I asked.

"I was so young, I barely remember," Señorita

Molina said. "It was toward the end of 1972. I developed an infection in my spine and had to spend the whole year at San Jorge Children's Hospital. That's in San Juan. There was a *medica mentos*—an antibiotic—that could have made the infection go away, but my family was very poor and could not afford a hundred dollars to pay for it."

"Is that why you have the wheelchair?" I asked.

"*Si*. Yes. Anyway, Mr. Clemente visited the hospital one day. He would do that all the time. There were no photographers or reporters there. He just did it because he cared. And he was so nice. The big baseball star—sitting at the edge of my bed! He told my parents that he was going to come back in a few weeks and give me a hundred-dollar bill so I could get the antibiotic I needed to get better. But he never did."

At that point, I could see Señorita Molina's eyes were wet. It occurred to me that maybe I never should have asked her about the candle.

"Why do you think he didn't come back?" I asked.

"Because *se murio*. He died, Tito."

Señorita Molina dabbed her eyes with a tissue and told me what happened. On December 23, 1972, there was a huge earthquake in Nicaragua, which is in Central America. It just about leveled the capital city, Managua. 350 square blocks were flattened. Two hospitals were destroyed. The main fire station collapsed. 5,000 people died, and 250,000 were left homeless, with no water or electricity.

Señorita Molina told me that Roberto Clemente had played winter baseball in Nicaragua and grew to love the people there. He wanted to help. So he organized a relief effort in Puerto Rico to get food, medicine, and clothing for the survivors of the earthquake. And he personally paid for a plane to fly the supplies to Nicaragua. He even insisted on going on the plane himself to make sure the stuff got to the people who needed it.

At that point, Señorita Molina cried as she pulled a yellowed newspaper clipping out of her desk drawer and showed it to me.

"It was *La Noche Vieja*—New Year's Eve," Señorita Molina told me. "The plane was loaded with 40,000 pounds of cargo, more than it was supposed to carry. The pilot was sleep deprived and in danger of losing his license. The crew was unqualified. There were mechanical problems too. The plane was only *volano* . . . how do you say . . . airborne for two minutes before it crashed into the ocean. Five people died, including Mr. Clemente."

"I'm sorry," I told her.

I didn't know what else to say.

"*La Noche Vieja* is one of the biggest nights of the year in Puerto Rico," she told me. "Mr. Clemente left his wife and three young sons that night to help the earthquake victims. He was not looking for publicity or fame. It was a mission of mercy. In Spanish—as you should know, Tito—the word '*clemente*' means 'merciful.'"

I felt like it was time for me to go. I thanked Señorita Molina for giving me the chance to bring up my grade.

But after I left the classroom, I stopped dead in my tracks in the hallway. An idea popped into my head.

I could stop it!

I could go back in time and make sure Roberto Clemente didn't get on that plane.

I could save his life.